***With an explosion of glass, and a
howl like some supernatural wind,
the French doors burst inward . . .***

Marianna's body was flung at Brady, knocking
him down. Above the roar of wind, he heard three
unearthly screams, and recognized the voices of
his family. He tried to see them, to shout their
names, but a dark shape struck him in the face,
and a second figure kicked out at him, taking the
breath from his body with a sickeningly painful
blow to his stomach.

Shapes moved all about, dark men in dark robes,
their faces the hideous reflections of animals, a
leering goat, a glitter-eyed hawk . . .

Helpless, unable to cry out, Dan Brady watched as
his wife's naked body was flung between two of
the robed figures, then forced to the floor.

"Mark her."

Charter books by Robert Faulcon

NIGHT HUNTER

coming soon:

NIGHT HUNTER 2: THE TALISMAN
NIGHT HUNTER 3: THE GHOST DANCE

NIGHT HUNTER

Robert Faulcon

CHARTER BOOKS, NEW YORK

NIGHT HUNTER

A Charter Book/published by arrangement with
the author

PRINTING HISTORY
Charter edition/July 1987

ISBN: 0-441-57469-6

Charter Books are published by The Berkley Publishing Group,
200 Madison Avenue, New York, New York 10016.
PRINTED IN THE UNITED STATES OF AMERICA

To Suey, Judith, Peter and Dan the Man,
With affection.

— PROLOGUE —

IT TOOK JUST five seconds for the woman to walk briskly past the broad frontage of the restaurant. She held on to her shoulder bag with both hands, walking with a slight stoop. As she passed the window she turned and glanced quickly back along the road.

She was a woman pursued and could not hide the fact.

The five seconds, and that furtive hindwards glance, were all that the man who sat just inside the restaurant needed. He recognized her at once.

"Christ! That's Ellen!"

He became aware of the ripple of laughter in the half-full coffee shop, and glanced around in embarrassment. Five or six youthful faces regarded him in amusement.

Conscious of a healthy glow in his face, he reached for his coat and briefcase, then stepped quickly out into the chill spring air.

This area of London was quite unfamiliar to him; he knew Oxford Street, and Charing Cross Road, and the various side streets in the region of the University buildings near Senate House. But Islington was just a name to him, a reference on the Monopoly board. He didn't know much of London at all, living as he did in the quiet suburbs of Sussex. It was his work for the Ennean Institute of Paranormal Research that had brought him to this bustling East London thoroughfare. He had interviewed a man who claimed clairvoyant powers (and who patently possessed no powers at all, save those of persuasion) and had come to the steamy, unpleasant restaurant for coffee, a cheese sandwich, and a few moments of debate as to how he would spend the rest of the afternoon.

And Ellen Bancroft, who had disappeared six months ago, had walked right past him, out of nowhere, out of memory . . .

And now out of sight.

It was market day, and the broad carriageway at the junction of Pentonville Road and Upper Street was a confusion of cars, buses and lorries, not to mention pedestrians surging like a mob towards the market stalls. He searched the crowds frantically for Ellen, following swiftly along the route she had taken.

By the time he had spotted her again, and was in hailing distance of her, he was quite breathless. He had to stop, doubling up for a moment and drawing breath deeply into his lungs before he could manage a cry of "Ellen! Ellen Bancroft!"

The way she turned round was like a beast of prey cornered, eyes wide, face registering some awful fear. At fifty yards distance she couldn't have failed to recognize him, but she turned away and began to run.

"What the devil . . .?"

He picked up his case, trying to forget about the pain in his side, and sprinted up the road, managing to call her name again and cursing himself for his unfit condition.

She stopped abruptly, turned very slowly and let him catch up with her. They were opposite the pink façade of a cinema, next to the iron railings of a tiny park. He leaned against the fence and tried to smile as he caught his breath. He was in his forties, out of condition, and was now quite flushed. But he ceased to worry about his own discomfort; rather, he found himself shocked and distressed to observe this woman who had once been so close to him.

"What do you want, David? Are you following me?" Her words were cold, hostile.

He stood upright, shaking his head. Such anger when there had been such affection; such anger after so many months of disappearance.

When she had first come to England, from University in

Boston, she had been a full-figured, dusky-skinned woman, with sparkling brown eyes and rich, black hair, hair that had framed a face as shapely and perfect as any he had seen in his life. To have seen Ellen Bancroft without a smile touching her lips was to have seen her (most likely) unconscious. She was cheerful, companionable and chatty, and she and David Marchant had been lovers; but she had settled with another man, and one not connected with the Ennean Institute, and had had a child by him.

Now, just six months after the last time Marchant had seen her, she was hollow-faced and her eyes were rimmed with the dark lines of anxiety and fatigue; her hair was streaked with grey; her breath was stale; she stood before him, shaking, not with rage, nor with fear, but with something that seemed to consist of a little of both. A woman going rapidly and pathetically to seed.

"Ellen," he said, as his heart calmed down and his breathing became easier, "Ellen, where on earth have you been?"

"What do you *want*, David?"

"Just to talk. It's been six months or more . . . Everyone's upset by the way you just disappeared, Geoffrey Dean . . ."

She spat the name back at him, contemptuous, angry. He had forgotten the strained relationship between Ellen and her supervisor. "We're just worried about you, Ellen. Elizabeth Smallwood, John Stanchell, all your old friends."

"Enough!" she shouted at him, her face a mask of irritation. Her gaze shifted restlessly past him. She clutched her shoulder bag even tighter, trying to turn it away from Marchant.

"What's happened to you, Ellen? You look so ill . . ."

"Fuck off, David!" she said violently, and turned away, stopping only when he reached out and grabbed her arm.

Furiously she swung on him, stared at him hard, and said with careful, angry words, "Go away, David. I beg you. For *your* sake, for *my* sake, just *leave me alone*! Forget you've seen me; forget me. If you keep following me . . ." a veiled threat, or an unspoken warning, he couldn't be sure, but he sensed behind the words a quality of desperation which told of her regret that she could not behave naturally with a man who had once been her lover.

He said, "Let me help, Ellen. Let me help you . . ."

"You fool! I'm beyond help! *You* know what happened, to Michael, to Justin . . ."

"It was cruel. I know that. But you can't hide away for ever. Your friends are desperate to help, but you've—"

He stopped speaking. Her gaze had gone beyond him, her eyes widening with what he took to be shock. He immediately looked round: a busy street, people with shopping, young couples, children. There was a traffic jam at the lights; a faded yellow Datsun had broken down and three spikey-haired youths were helping to push it up onto the pavement, out of the way of the crush of cars and vans.

All this he took in at a glance. But when he stared back at Ellen she seemed shocked, then angry, and before he could say more than, "What is it?" she had shouted, "You bastard! You're one of them . . . you've led it here!"

She began to run, away from him, away from the traffic. Marchant followed her and in five long strides had caught her up and stopped her in her flight. "Ellen, *please!*"

"Oh Christ!" she shrieked, staring beyond him. The look she gave him, then, was one of total contempt, a contempt which shifted into uncertainty, then resolve: her right hand slapped across his face, the nails turned in so that his skin was scratched with two inch-long lines. He clutched his cheek, felt the sticky warmth of blood, and was too stunned to do or say anything as Ellen raced away from him, hair flying, her arms awkwardly positioned as she struggled to run and keep hold of her bag.

Marchant turned again to see what had frightened her. He saw only ordinary people, doing ordinary things; the blood cooled on his cheek and he began to feel pain. He noticed that there was something pungent about the smell of that blood, as if she had smeared some chemical, or herb on his skin. He stared hard into the distance, wondering who had so terrified Ellen Bancroft.

She had left the main street, darting down a narrow passageway between the shops, and emerging into a wide square where four-story houses rose steeply all around. Many of the flats, here, were empty, the buildings being run-down and often semi-derelict. The smell that hung in the air was of refuse, left for weeks without collection. It was an area of dereliction in sharp—and poignant!—contrast to the general belief that Islington was an "in" part of the city, and had been attractively modernized; the *nouveau chic* had its areas of desolation.

Ellen was walking swiftly from the square. Marchant briskly pursued her, but half-way across he stopped, turned and stared at the empty passageway.

He could have sworn that someone had walked through behind him and called to him.

A woman came trotting down the steps from one of the houses, glanced at him, and scurried off towards the shops through the passage, unbothered by any person or persons unseen. Marchant was glad of that touch of normality. But something had disturbed him, either Ellen's strange behaviour, or something else . . .

As he walked from the square he felt his face go quite cold, his heart begin to race. The sensation of being followed was quite appalling.

Without really thinking of where he was headed, Marchant found himself in an area of garages, behind two blocks of flats. Across the courtyard an iron fire-escape rose up the side of a building close at hand and he could see Ellen's distraught figure rapidly climbing the stairs to an apartment some way above ground. She disappeared from sight.

He began to walk towards Ellen's apartment block, but to his surprise found his legs went weak, eventually refusing to move forward. He took a step back and tried again, but as he passed a certain point his head grew dizzy, his limbs went weak, and he was forced to retrace his steps to avoid fainting. His body was wet, soaking his shirt and trousers. He noticed that his hands were shaking.

Standing quite still, and staring up at the higher windows of the block, he called Ellen's name, and eventually thought he saw a curtain twitch on the third floor. "Ellen. Please let me talk to you. Please!"

Behind him, someone took four quick steps towards him, and he turned in shock, half thinking that he was about to be attacked.

●   ●   ●

At the sound of the first scream an old lady came to the window of her flat and watched in shocked astonishment as the struggling body of a man was apparently blown high into the air, higher than the flats themselves. There was a persistent and agonized ululation of terror from the thrashing figure, which fell heavily back to the concreted roadway and began to crawl towards the fire-escape.

As if a sudden wind had gusted, and the man weighed no more than a leaf, he was blown across the courtyard through mid-air, body turning head-over-heels and smashing hard against a garage door. A moment later his clothes were shredded from his body, cast into the wind like tatters of coloured paper. The old lady choked on her own gorge as the naked man's head twisted completely round on its shoulders and the broken body ceased to struggle forever.

— ONE

LATER, HE WOULD think back to these cold, frantically busy days before Christmas and try to discern, among the chaos of experiments and travel and meetings, some clue as to what had happened, some hint as to the beginning of the tragedy that would soon sweep through his life.

At the age of thirty-five Daniel Brady was fully immortal. A tall, leanly-built man in the full flush of health, and with a secure and challenging research position in the Ministry of Defence at Hillingvale, he could no more have seriously contemplated his own mortality than he could have changed the flow of time. Death, if certainly a reality to him, was nevertheless a reality one step removed, something that happened to others. It was not a consideration that he applied to himself, or to his young wife, Alison, or to his two growing children. His concerns were for work, for the research project that was only giving very tentative results, and for his new house in Berkshire which was too big, too cold, and probably a very ill-considered buy; and his youngest child, six-year-old Marianna, was not settling in at school, and neither he nor Alison could understand why.

Worries about his family intruded upon the concentration necessary for him to conduct his research properly; concerns for his research likewise affected him at home: during the rainy autumn he had been broody, distant, distracted. He was well aware that results were essential in his line of work, and in particular in this place of work that had so readily accepted him from University, ten years before. The Ministry of Defence had small research installations scattered over the length and breadth of Britain. It was considered a considerable achievement to be invited to work in one of them. It was very common indeed for a man or woman to leave the Ministry's employ after two or three unsuccessful years.

Three days before Christmas Dan Brady had set up his study for one last attempt to get some results in the old year, prior to despairingly closing down the action until January 3rd. In the months to come, when he would have ample opportunity to contemplate these last happy, if frustrating days, he would see the first hint that at that time he had already been "marked."

"Are we ready to go?"

Brady sat before two green-tinted screens, watching the solid-line traces upon one and the regular, wavy patterns on the other. In a small, enclosed cage a sullen looking female fat-tailed gerbil sat watching the blank walls of her environment. She couldn't see Brady, not could she hear, nor smell, nor feel vibration through the wall of her prison. Brady's sole contact with her was through the cerebellar trace on the screen; the animal's hindbrain was active, and actively registering.

The young man who worked as Brady's research assistant made some final adjustments to the various pieces of equipment, then sat down at his own station and called, "Ready." He was thin and willowy, his eyes framed by huge, silver rimmed spectacles. He wore the white coat of a lab technician, whereas Brady was dressed informally, casually (his department supervisor said scruffily) in a voluminous roll neck, and grey cord slacks. Brady hated formality, and the formal attire of the laboratory.

He leaned forward and peered beyond a glass screen into a strange landscape . . .

It was night and the desert was cold. There was no moon, but an eerie light picked out the shapes of boulders, stubby cactus, and the solitary, upright shape of an animal, feeding nervously on a locust. The creature was small and rat-like, its feet abnormally long, and it balanced precariously in the danger-filled darkness, ready to flee at the first hint of attack. *Pachyuromys duprasi* was a natave of deserts in East Africa; a nocturnal predator of locusts, spiders and other night-feeding creatures it was, itself, the natural prey of the sand cat.

Into this tiny desert, bordered not by the lusher vegetation of a river terrace, or by high, snow-capped mountains, but rather by perspex walls darkened to allow the illusion of night, into this miniature world the first danger came.

The sand cat betrayed its stealthy approach by the faintest of drumming on the reverberant sand. The gerbil straightened, ceased chewing, then peered to the right and the left through wide, shining eyes. The cat leapt towards it in an instant, but the gerbil was faster: it bounded across the dry, chill landscape until it fetched up against the invisible wall across its territory.

The pursuit was not continued; the cat was illusory, generated by the research assistant from across the environment.

But in that single instant of escape something happened fifty yards distant, where Brady sat watching the screens, and the imprisoned female animal. First, on the broader of the two screens, which showed four single, unbroken traces, a tiny, almost fleeting peak of activity had occurred. On the smaller screen, which showed the cerebellar activity of the female gerbil, three powerful, sustained peaks registered a dramatic change in the unconscious awareness of the tiny animal.

Out of sight of her mate, unaware of the danger, the female's own hindbrain had registered the input of a warning signal; not by sound, nor by sight, nor by vibration; an extrasensory signal had been relayed from brain to brain, and then to machinery; a warning signal that had been observed!

Brady sat back in his chair and allowed himself the luxury of a thin smile, a token gesture of self-congratulation. "What did we get?" called the assistant, and Brady said, "A hint . . . just a hint. The female registered the warning very powerfully, but our own detectors spotted something too. Just a hint . . ."

"Stronger than Trial 17?"

"Maybe not. But a damn sight stronger than nothing at all!"

The wiry young man beamed his pleasure. They'd got two results, then, out of forty trials. They'd repeated their result, and surely now it was just a question of refining the equipment until it was sensitive enough to clearly pick up the electro-magnetic output of the frightened animal.

"And that," said Brady, beginning to rise from his chair, "is that until the New Year. Close down for Christmas . . ."

He had been about to say more, but he stopped, feeling suddenly cold, suddenly chilled. He straightened and looked around, wondering idly if cool air from the desert environment was leaking into the laboratory. A light flickered. The research assistant frowned, looked uneasily around. For some reason Brady stared at the oscilloscope screens, at the single lines that showed the machine's own mechanical unresponsiveness, and at the fluctuating output from the brain of the female gerbil.

And quite suddenly the signals went haywire.

"Good God, come and look at this!"

Brady leaned forward on the console, watching the trace from the gerbil peak and race, the animal cowering in a corner of its box, staring vaguely upwards and outwards, the leads from the skull probes tangled around its tiny body.

"Something's scared the hell out of it . . . *and* the other!"

In the desert the gerbil was racing in energetic circles; the mechanical trace, for all its insensitivity, was registering an output of electro-magnetic energy of such strength that the signal was too large for the screen.

In the eerie silence Brady stared first at the machinery, then at the animals. Finally, the signals on the smaller screen became single, straight lines; the animals had died.

"Well I'm damned," he said. "That's the first time . . . what the hell could have caused that?"

He got no answer from the technician. Brady pulled the sleeves of his jumper down his arms, feeling cold and shivery. For no reason that he could identify he felt afraid, the laboratory becoming claustrophobic, threatening.

He turned and left the room, his heart racing, his mind registering nothing but a strong, almost violent urge to get away from the place.

As he fairly shot into the corridor, ignoring his jacket which hung just inside the laboratory door, he realized that his Section Chief, Andrew Haddingham, was strolling easily towards him, looking half puzzled, half amused. Haddingham was in thoughtful conversation with the lean, greying figure of the Department Superintendent, George Campbell. Campbell was a sour-faced Scot, a man who had little tolerance for the personal side of his employees' lives. He frowned as he witnessed Brady's slight dishevelment, and clamped his teeth on his unlit pipe in a gesture of annoyance.

"What's the matter, Dan?" said Haddingham with a smile, as the three men met. "You look spooked."

Brady nodded, and tried a slight grin back. He was aware of Campbell's intense, disapproving scrutiny. *Dammit, he thought, at least I'm still working seriously this close to the holidays.*

He liked Haddingham, though, and got on well with the plump man. Haddingham was only slightly younger than the Supervisor, perhaps fifty-five, but he was far younger at heart and had an enthusiasm for ideas and projects that could spark even the dullest of the Ministry minds. Unmarried, and rather private about his past, Haddingham was a regular visitor at Brady's home.

"A touch of claustrophobia," Brady said, and glanced at Campbell. "Been stuck in the laboratory a few hours too many."

Campbell, to Brady's surprise, allowed a genuine smile to touch his lips; his grey eyes flashed with something approaching pleasure. "Good to see you working so hard, Mister Brady," he said. "I hope we'll be seeing some positive results from you in the coming year. Excuse me gentlemen, I have a train . . ."

Campbell walked off, left hand in the pocket of his grey suit jacket. Brady stared after him, then glanced at Haddingham and laughed wearily. "Never lets up, does he?"

"Not on anybody, Dan," said Haddingham, running a hand through his unkempt brown hair. "I feel shell shocked myself, just now. Been hauled over the coals for the whole department."

"His way of saying Happy Christmas," grinned Brady. "I'd buy you a drink, but my house is a disaster zone . . ."

He was about to turn away and fetch his jacket when Haddingham tugged at his arm, questioned the younger man with his gaze, then said, "You really *are* spooked, Dan. What happened in there?"

Brady hesitated just a second before deciding not to tell the other man what had occurred . . . not yet. "Got a strange result, that's all. I'll tell you about it next year."

"A strange result sends you running scared from the room? What is it, Dan?"

Brady shrugged, disliking Haddingham's sudden intensity, the way he was intuiting Brady's genuine sense of fear. "As I said, claustrophobia, too close to Christmas . . . it really *is* nothing Andrew. I'm on edge, that's all."

Haddingham shrugged, smiled and reached out a hand to the younger man. "Happy Christmas to you, then, Dan. And to the family. Enjoy yourselves . . ."

"We shall. First Christmas in a new home; got to make it something special."

It had really been Alison who had fallen in love with the house at Brook's Corner, that previous March. Their town house in West London had suddenly—for no perceptible reason—become too small; it was perhaps because of Marianna's great enthusiasm for "projects," involving cutting paper, using clay, and sticking bits and pieces of disposable carton and package to make buildings and cars, all of which meant that living rooms, bedrooms, even bathrooms, became cluttered and untidy. And with Dominick wanting to have a room where he could bring back his friends and play music at exceptionally loud volumes (he was eleven, but had already discovered more than twenty forms of contemporary rhythm and blues), Brady had, on impulse, decided to sell and move his family westwards, to the area around Pinewood, where houses could either be of exceptional expense, or of very reasonable price.

They had been directed to the house at Brook's Corner because, at seventy-five thousand pounds, it would not stretch them that much, even though it was in need of considerable decoration. Alison Brady had taken one look at the place and adored it. Dan Brady himself was the sort of man who could be happy anywhere that his family were happy. The house struck him as too large, too cold and too isolated, but Alison's rapture at the thought of living there was overwhelming. While the children had chased about the overgrown, partly wooded grounds (over an acre!) he and Alison had come to the decision to buy, to paint three of the rooms, and to leave the greater part of the needed modernization for a year or so while they saved a little capital.

They had moved in in June, and made a presentable lawn at the back, gravelled the driveway at the front, and found that rapidly, almost inevitably, they had expanded—as a family— to fill every nook and cranny of the place.

Brook's Corner was just ten miles from the Ministry of Defence Institute at Hillingvale, where Brady worked, and he drove those ten miles, now, fast and without due care to the conditions of the road. He half hoped Alison would be home, but she was conscientious, and very much involved with two MSc projects at the College where she worked, and from years of experience Brady knew that she would only take off the day before Christmas Eve, and would work on in her department until such time as her students would relinquish her.

He was not surprised, then, to find the house in darkness. It was four in the afternoon, a gloomy, bitterly cold day, and the central heating was off—one of the children fiddling with it, no doubt. Briskly he turned the radiators on, then poured himself a gin with tonic, going into the lounge where he set a log fire, but refrained from lighting it. In the corner of the lounge the Christmas tree was an immense forest of a structure, rising to the ceiling, shedding needles in spiky layers, and half covered with a mess of tinsel and coloured streamers— Marianna's ineffective attempt to decorate the tree, and an effort that would have to be discreetly corrected before Christmas Eve itself.

Both Marianna and Dominick were at the Newmans' (causing havoc, no doubt) and Alison would pick them up on her way home from the college. That would be within a few minutes, so Brady took the opportunity to relax, feet up on one of the armchairs, gin and tonic freshened, a well-creased copy of *Omni* propped up before him.

At four thirty it began to rain, the windows shaking slightly with the driving force of the dusk wind. The lounge was large and not yet completely draughtproof and Brady shivered as a cool breeze tickled his neck. Fragments of leaf that had been caught in the chimney fell into the grate, startling him. He got up, draining his drink, and glanced at his watch.

Alison was very late. They should all have been home some time before.

As he was about to pick up the phone to call the Newmans, it rang; Alison was on the line. "Dan? It's Alison. Listen, I'm really stuck here. Probably for an hour . . ."

"An hour! Oh for God's sake . . ."

"It can't be helped. I'm behind with my own work. Pete Wright's project took a lot of reading. I've only just finished with him."

Brady felt a touch of irritation. He was rapidly trying to get into the spirit of the impending Christmas, and very much wanted to spend time this evening tidying the tree, and getting the last paper-chains slung in the downstairs rooms. He was finished with Hillingvale for the rest of the year, and chauvinistically felt a touch of resentment that Alison wouldn't finish with her own work place with equal enthusiasm.

"Never mind," he said. "Get home as quickly as you can. I'll get supper going. How about the kids?"

"Could you pick them up? The Newmans will be screaming murder by now. Would you mind?"

"Okay. Hurry home."

Before he left he set the log fire alight, so that they would all come home to a cosy lounge. It was only a twenty minute round trip to John Newman's.

And he wouldn't stay for a drink.

Alison almost called Dan right back again, just to say that there was cold pork to be used up for supper that evening, and before they started on anything else, but she refrained. Dan hated her to fuss about the house and kitchen, liking to share the responsibility for all those drab and irritating chores that make a household run smoothly. He was a good cook, if one of erratic inclination, and their only real point of difference in the kitchen (in twelve years of marriage) was that Dan tended to cook extravagantly, and in quantities more suited to a barracks than a family of four, whereas Alison practiced a frugality instilled upon her by both her childhood, and her year in Kenya.

She left her small second-floor office, turning out the light as she did so, and walked briskly along the corridor to the extensive library. She only really needed an hour to cross-check three references for her paper (with Pete Wright) on zonal agriculture on clay-based river terraces, but she wanted to get it done before tonight because she knew that tomorrow—the last day before the Christmas break for the staff—there would be no work possible in the atmosphere of drunken boisterousness.

On the way to the library she picked up her coat, ready to leave as soon as possible.

Alison Brady was thirty-four years old, a sprightly, energetic woman, thin to the point of being skinny, but content to be so because she loathed the idea of fat people, and of becoming plump and unfit herself. She was a sports fanatic, playing at least half an hour's badminton every day, and was increasingly scornful of Dan for neglecting his body so much.

Like husband Dan, Alison was an informal dresser, preferring jeans and a jumper to tailored skirts and blouses; but there was an elegance about her that made her always seem perfectly dressed for any occasion. She wore her dark hair naturally wavy, and swept it back from her forehead; she knew the style suited her, and she was not by any means averse to the flattering attentions of her teenage male students.

In the library she dumped her coat and papers on one of the desks nearest to the door and walked into the complex of rows of books and journals to seek the three journals she wished to consult. Pete Wright was working busily at the back of the library, seemingly unexhausted by the marathon supervision session with his tutor that afternoon. There were no other students or staff in the library; of course not. It was three days to Christmas and only the workaholics were left.

Later, in the peace of her own house and lying still in the darkness, she would be able to remember the exact moment at which she had known someone else had entered the library. She hadn't *heard* anything, neither the door opening and shutting, nor a footfall; she hadn't seen anything, or smelled anything. It was a sensation as intangible and discrete as it was potent and certain. As she stood leafing through the *Journal of Industrial Agriculture* she just *knew* that a third party had entered the library, and was walking down the aisle of books towards her.

She didn't bother to look up, merely stood closer to the side of the narrow alleyway between the shelves to let the person pass. After a second or two she realised that he had stopped and was staring at her, and with just the slightest of unpleasant sensations on her skin she glanced round to see who it was.

"Oh God!"

The words came as involuntarily as the journal slipping from her fingers. The book hit the floor with a crash, and Alison reached down, confused and upset, to retrieve it. She looked both ways along the aisle. Her knees were like jelly, hardly able to support her weight as she walked slowly out from the bookshelves, frightened and disturbed by her *certain* knowledge that someone had walked up behind her.

The student was gone. She was alone in the library. The room was empty, cold, and musty with the smell of old journals; rain beat noisily against the high windows; wind shook the overhead strip-lights.

She placed her journals on one of the tables and sat down, her hands shaking, her whole body trembling with fright. She stared across the room at the journal-shelves, and the dark, deserted gangways between them.

Somewhere in that stillness the pages of a book were noisily turned, as if blown in a wind. A moment later there was silence again.

But as Alison listened to the heavy silence, and stared at the shelves of books, she could not shake off the idea—powerfully felt—that someone was standing in the nearest aisle, intently and deliberately watching her.

─ *Two* ─────────────────────────

"I'VE FINISHED THEM!" came the voice from the hallway, and a moment later the lounge door was noisily and awkwardly opened and tiny Marianna entered, smiling with triumph and achievement.

From his precarious position, half-way up a step-ladder next to the Christmas tree, Brady said, "Well *done*, that strange-looking child!"

"I'm *not* strange-looking!" she said adamantly, as she carried her tray of papier-maché crib figures across the room to the fireside. The tray was so big that the girl could hardly walk with it. Alison rose to help her. Brady climbed down from the ladder, glad of the opportunity for a pause in the back-breaking work of decorating the tree. His daughter literally reeked of paint, he noticed, as he sat down beside her.

"What are *those*?" said Dominick, peering at Marianna's creations. "Crib figures! They're more like aliens."

"You're just jealous," said the girl, with as much contempt as she could muster, then grinned with satisfaction as she settled back on her haunches and surveyed her handiwork.

At the age of six (and two-thirds, she would insist) Marianna Brady was the smallest, skinniest definition of human chaos that her father could bring to mind. She was spider thin, and could never keep her socks above an untidy bunch around each ankle; her print dresses hung on her like tents. In the last

year or so her raucous behaviour had initiated, slightly early,
the growing-up process by which milk-teeth become replaced
with stronger, more adult dentition; her mouth, if pretty, was
a disaster zone of gaps, which she hid with her left hand when
giggling, but which she only disguised because Dominick
teased her. He teased her more about her spectacles, a tiny,
round-framed pair of corrective lenses that the family had
nick-named "granny glasses." She was slightly short-sighted
in her left eye, although her right eye was perfectly strong.

When she moved through the house she was incapable of
walking; her spindly form would clatter up stairs and through
the rooms in search of raw materials for her various projects,
or pursuing one of the Brady's two patient, but rather war-
torn cats.

Despite the gappy smile, she was immensely pretty, and
Daniel Brady's favourite child (oh yes, he would acknowledge
a favourite . . . to himself.) He even loved her when she strad-
dled his lap and twisted his nose as "punishment" for making
her always go to bed before she'd finished whatever game she
was playing, or whatever model she was making. Artistically
she was very talented, as was evidenced by the set of crib-
characters. If Brady had been slightly apprehensive as to what
shapes and sizes would emerge from the chaotic focus of
Marianna's industry—her appalliingly untidy room—he was
glad at least that she had the power to concentrate on a project
until it was done, and to achieve personal satisfaction from
her creativity.

Dominick Brady, four years older than his sister, was a contrast in style and appearance to his sister as dramatic as it was
complete. A tall, sensitive child, big-framed and destined to
grow into a giant of a man, he was shy to the point of exasper-
ation. Not at home, of course, where his voice echoed re-
soundingly around the spacious house in strong competiton
with Marianna's, but in company it would take the better part
of an hour to extract conversation from him.

Neither Dan nor Alison Brady believed in forcing a child to
change its natural personality, and Dom's shyness was never
drawn attention to. They would simply involve him in chats
and discussions in a natural way and treat him no differently
when he was garrulous than when he was painfully unable to

express words through the embarrassment of flushed, tongue-tied nervousness. By this simple process of not allowing Dominick to become self-conscious of his own shyness he was gradually emerging from it.

If Dan Brady extended greater protection to his daughter, Alison was the sympathetic nest-mother to the boy. Marianna, of course, demanded and received the lion's share of attention from visitors, especially visitors who were strangers to the family. The slight seed of resentment, already sown in Dom's personality, might cause difficulty later in life, but at this pre-teens age his irritation manifested itself healthily in loud arguments, and bitter quarrels with his sister. Anger expressed was dissipated. The Bradys encouraged the vociferous exchange of frustration, even though it was painful to the ears.

There were no arguments that evening, three days before the 25th of December. The family gathered round to inspect the Virgin, her Spouse, and the Infant Jesus. Marianna remained kneeling by the wood fire and watched the inspection.

"Remarkable," observed Dan Brady, as he picked up an infant whose head was as large as his body, and whose expression owed more to the grinning Appalachian Mountain character who graced MAD magazine than to the serene smile of the Holy Infant. The child was—in relation to the size of its mother—practically fully grown, which no doubt explained the lopsided grimace on the Virgin Mary's face. The animals had walked out of science fiction, and one—the cow—was immediately nicknamed the C' Porker, since its features owed as much to the one animal as to the other. Wet paint rubbed off on the Bradys' fingers as the family expressed their genuine admiration of the characters.

"What about the three wise men?" demanded Dominick.

"I didn't have time," said Marianna defensively.

Brady said, "They probably followed the wrong star. They'll be here next Christmas."

Dominick carried the figures across to the model theatre that had been converted into a stable, and Alison and Dan Brady watched in silent satisfaction as the two children played with the several characters within that miniature world.

"Fingers crossed for a peaceful Christmas," said Alison, stretching her feet out to the fire.

"Some hope."

Later, when the children were in bed, Alison told Brady of her scary encounter in the library. She was still shaken by it, still a little on edge.

"Is the library haunted?"

"I don't know," she said. "Perhaps it is. That's the third time in a month that I've felt spooked."

"Anybody else encountered it?"

Alison nestled against him, warm and sleepy. "Don't think so. It really unnerved me, Dan. I mean, normally I'd just shake it off, put it down to a windy night, fatigue, too much adrenaline pumping through my system keeping me alert, But . . ."

She didn't finish. Brady stroked her hair and her shoulders, trying to soothe the tension he could feel in her muscles. She wriggled slightly with pleasure.

"It's funny," he said. "I had a fright today as well."

"What happened?"

"The EM detectors went haywire. One scope was connected up to a female gerbil, reading bio-electrical output from its hindbrain—the location of instinctive action and sensitivity. The other was just trying to pick up ES signals out of the air . . ."

"ES? Oh, Extra Sensory. I didn't think you could do that yet?"

"We got a minute trace today. Enough to keep Campbell happy. Anyway something spooked both animals, and the response was incredible. It had to be fear, and it got to me too. The only other time I've known something happen like that was when we were getting interference from subsonic signalling. But if this was a stray signal it must have been damned powerful. Gerbils are tough, and the female was killed by its own fright reaction . . ."

"How horrible." Alison straightened, stared at Dan censoriously. "I still don't see how you can work with animals. It's grotesque."

"I don't dissect them."

"You just scare them half to death."

"I don't scare them a tenth as much as they get scared in the natural habitat. And they never get eaten . . ."

"That's what you say." Alison settled back against him. "But I know you MOD people; can't talk about what you really do . . . I'm sure it's a lot worse."

Brady laughed. "Funny, isn't it. My work is classified; all work at Hillingvale is classified; and there's absolutely nothing going on there that could be of the slightest interest to anyone."

"Likely story." Alison climbed to her feet, tugged down her jumper and smiled at Dan. "I'm ready for bed."

"But it's early. Not ten yet . . ."

"I said I'm ready for bed, Dan." She reached out her hand and Brady smiled as he took it, allowing himself to be hauled upright out of his comfortable armchair. The wood fire was burning low, and would be safe to leave, now. They kissed fondly in front of the glowing embers, then walked slowly upstairs, arms round each other.

And they had not been in bed for more than five minutes when Marianna began to scream.

"Oh God, not again!" Alison pushed Dan away roughly, and swung her legs out of the covers.

"It never bloody fails, does it?" Brady was both irritable and frustrated, and he pulled on his long, winter robe before walking quickly to Marianna's room. But if frustration tainted his words with anger, both he and Alison were edgy with concern for their daughter's mental health and these nightmares were becoming ridiculously frequent.

Brady practically ran into the girl's room and switched on the light, blinking against the sudden brilliance. He wrinkled his nostrils at the unpleasant smell in the place. Marianna's cries had died away to a whimper, and he saw her, crouched in the corner, behind the cluttered desk. Her knees were drawn up to her chest, and she was clutching her Paddington Bear to her body, burying her face in its hat. "All right darling," said Brady gently, picking her up and carrying her from the room. "It was just a dream . . ."

Marianna was shaking, her eyes filled with tears, but not expressing her fear with any show of sobbing. She held onto her father tightly and when they were downstairs, in front of the dying fire, she curled up in his lap and allowed him to soothe her. Alison made a small glass of warm milk, then came in and sat down by her daughter, reaching out to brush stray hairs from the child's face.

"She seems all right now," said Brady.

"I don't like him," said Marianna weakly, and Brady and Alison exchanged glances. "He frightens me. And he *smells*!"

"Who does, darling?" asked Alison quietly. "Who frightens you?"

"The man. The Smokey Man. I don't like him."

She snuggled more tightly against Brady's chest. "What did he do, lovely?" he asked. "Did he come into the room?"

"He looked at me, up close. I was frightened. He *smells*!"

To Alison, Brady mouthed the question, "Did you smell anything?"

"Yes, quite powerfully, like rotting vegetation. The window was open, but it couldn't have been the pond, could it?"

"I don't think so." He rocked Marianna back and forth. Alison continued to stroke her, and soon the violent trembling in the girl's body died away. "Did he touch you?"

The girl shook her head. "He frightens me. He just looks down at me and smiles, then he runs away."

Marianna's encounters with the Smokey Man were becoming bothersome. Dominick, at her age, had also suffered from a recurring nightmare, but one that involved falling. It had taken him a year to outgrow the dreaming phase. Now Marianna, almost certainly in her sleep, was regularly encountering a figure that she described as "smokey," a tenuous, drifting shape, that sometimes smelled and sometimes didn't. This was the fourth encounter, and it seemed to have been less intense and less intensely frightening than before. The first time she had dreamed of the apparition the girl had jumped from her window and floundered into the pond. It had given Brady bad dreams for weeks, and they had covered the pond with a stiff, wire grating.

As on previous occasions, Brady was inclined to assume the figure had been a dream; but tonight because of his own discomforting experience during the day—and Alison's haunting in the library—they sat there for a long while, not willing to acknowledge that nothing had really happened.

Could the house be haunted? It was over a hundred years old, a remote, rambling, five-bedroomed place, and presumably it had had its fair share of history. But would a haunting presence follow the house's occupants to *work*?

"What the hell's happening to us?" Brady said softly, and Alison shrugged.

"Nothing that can't be explained by overwork, too much to do on the house, and natural parental tension just before Christmas." She smiled. "We're on edge . . ." she simplified.

"Yes, I guessed that's what you meant." Brady shifted Marianna's sleepy form on his lap, and she sat up and stared at him, her gaze flickering from one eye to the other. "Time to go back to bed," he said.

"I'm scared. I want to sleep in your bed tonight."

"Well you can't. And there's no point arguing. The Smokey Man was a bad dream, and now he's gone."

Marianna pinched her lips together and reached out to twist Brady's nose with her left hand. "He might still be there . . ."

"Then we'd better send Willy Crinkleleaf with you, to make sure. Where are you Willy? Brady looked round. "Ah, there you are."

"*Where*'s Willy Crinkleleaf?" Marianna peered over Brady's shoulder, smiling.

"He's right there, by the fire," he pointed to thin air then waved. Marianna waved as well. "Sorry to drag you out of your Oak Tree, Willy."

"Sorry Willy," said Marianna. She climbed off Brady's lap, then looked at him. "Won't you come up with me, Daddy?"

"Certainly not. Off you go, and Willy Crinkleleaf will be right behind you. And if that old Smokey Man's in the room, well, you'll kick him out the window, won't you Willy? You'll hear a big splash in the pond."

Marianna giggled, then ran quickly for the stairs, calling, "Come on Willy."

An imaginative child, Marianna adored such friendly sprites as Willy Crinkleleaf, who lived in the oak at the end of the lawn, and Tim Tarrabob, who lived under the garden and was forever pulling weeds downwards just as Brady got to them to hoe them up. Brady's own father had used such elementals of nature to describe and teach the environment; and of course, they made great stories. Marianna, with her childish fear of the dark and her capacity to dream of more sinister supernatural forces, benefited marvellously from inhabiting her world—just peripherally—with more benign spirits. It had done Brady no psychological harm—except, perhaps, to give him a deep and abiding passion for fantasy stories—and it could only do Marianna good as well.

With Willy Crinkleleaf as her guardian for going up the stairs, she would relax; in a few years, like Dom, she would become sceptical of these forest and earthly beasts. (Although Dominick, for all his ridiculing of stories about garden sprites, was not above setting the occasional trap for Willy Crinkleleaf. Twice Brady had found him erecting an elaborate system of string snares, and mazes formed from crushed herbs and chalk. Where he had found the details of these traps Brady had never discovered).

They sat in silence for a few minutes, listening as Marianna pattered about her room before bouncing into bed and (presumably) burying herself below the blankets.

"What a family," said Alison quietly, and moved across to the armchair where Brady sat. It was still warm in the lounge, the dying fire guttering as the last pieces of wood were consumed. Brady reached out and turned off the lamp behind his chair. In the glowing red fire-light Alison's skin was smooth and golden, and he leaned forward to kiss her cheeks, her nose, then her mouth. "Where were we?" he said, and she shrugged off her thin house-robe, undid the belt of his dressing gown, and pulled herself up so that she could lie upon him.

Brady touched her gently, stroking her back, her thighs, feeling her slim body move across him, then onto him. Her breasts, so small and firm in his hands, seemed excessively responsive tonight. Her own hands gripped his shoulders as she moved on him, her mouth on his mouth, stifling their regular, rhythmic murmurs as her passion, and his, increased.

The next morning Dominick was up at the crack of dawn, running through the house crying the word "Snow!" at the top of his lungs. Dan Brady had slept only fitfully, finally succumbing to unconsciousness at around four in the morning. As he forced his eyes open, and listened to the excited yelling of his son, he realized that he felt absolutely shattered.

Alison rose silently, dressed silently, walked silently and sleepily down to the kitchen to fix some coffee. Brady lay in bed, feeling cold and unwilling to rise. When Marianna finally bounded onto the bed, and shook him to attention, he gave up the ghost of a possibility that he might lie-in and allowed himself to be dragged to the window, to witness the wonder of nature that had sprinkled the garden.

It had been a light snow flurry, probably lasting only minutes, in that coldest part of the night just before dawn. But the garden was white, and the illusion of deep snow was at once wonderful (to the children) and horrifying (to Brady, who loathed snow).

Marianna's fear of the night before had vanished totally. She had slept well—as much as she ever slept—and now bounded around her room locating boots, scarves, jumpers, and thick slacks. By seven-thirty she and Dominick were scraping snow from the high, brick wall that surrounded the grounds on two sides, and lobbing fragile but highly effective snowballs at each other.

Their faces glowed with colour as they sat to breakfast soon after. Their disappointment on witnessing the snow layer vanish with advancing morning was almost comical. But in any case, there was more to be done today than just playing around in the garden . . .

All four of them drove to Uxbridge, Alison armed with one immense list of requirements for the next few days, Brady with a second. They split up, Brady taking Dom with him, and met up again two hours later, loaded down with boxes, bags and wrapped packages. Uxbridge was unbearably crowded, thousands of last minute shoppers struggling—just like the Bradys —to obtain the rapidly dwindling supplies that could carry them through to New Year.

They visited a Santa Claus grotto of course, Marianna threatening to leave home were she denied a chance to check her theory that the man who sat there wore a false beard, and wasn't the *real* Santa Claus at all. Point proven, and one angry Father Christmas left adjusting his torn stage props, the Bradys went to Iver to have lunch with Dan's sister, Rosemary.

Rosemary and Bill Suchock lived in more modest surround-

ings on a housing estate. Their single child was Marianna's
age, a shy, unpleasant lad who sought his own company, and
refused to speak to Dan and Alison at all. Dan Brady felt a
shiver of apprehension at the thought of Christmas Day, when
the three of them would be joining the fun at Brook's Corner.
Each year it was the same: by three in the afternoon little
Malcolm would be the focus of attention, agreeing to cease his
tantrum only if all other activity were ceased and the present
company made a fuss of him. Brady thought fondly of the
woodshed that he had inherited with Brook's Corner, and the
high carpenter's bench within it, and the thin, flexible lengths
of alder branch that would inflict such justifiable pain on such
a sullenly juvenile backside.

Maybe this year for the first time . . . maybe . . .

They were away from Iver by three; it grew gloomy so
rapidly, and the sky lowered and became threatening, snow
clouds building and a wind of such bitter chill springing up
that Brady felt cold even through his heavy army surplus
anorak.

Once back home though, Alison busied herself with un-
packing the day's purchases and storing them, while Brady
made up the fire, then took the children with him into the
garden to chop enough logs for four days, and gather some
thin sticks from around the small stand of dead elms that
separated Brook's Corner from the smaller house known as
Ravenshead. Brady refused to cut the trees down, dead though
they were. Their branches, skeletal and sinister, were a dramatic break against the skyline in both summer and winter. As
long as he checked the trees regularly for dangerous branches
he felt he could risk keeping the trunks standing for a few
years.

Tiny Marianna, arms loaded with green fringed sticks,
marched in and out of the house in her red wellington boots,
bulkily clad in one of Dominick's old padded jackets. Her
breath frosted in great clouds as she raced to and fro, gathering firewood. Dominick chopped and chopped at the heavier
wood, while Brady waited patiently, then gave one mighty
stroke of the axe himself to achieve the desired cut. The cats
watched them curiously from the warmth of the lounge, too

clever by half to go out into such a gloomy, icy afternoon.

At one point, as dusk grew deeper, Marianna found enough snow still lurking beneath two logs to make a snowball, and she crept up behind Brady, threw it so that it exploded against the back of his head as he was bent over, stacking logs, and then scampered—pursued—across the garden, climbing onto the roof of the woodshed with a nimbleness that almost seemed impossible in view of her boots and bulkily clothed figure. Standing there, just out of reach of him, she thumbed her nose and laughed at him, only breaking from her taunting as light flashed from behind.

Brady looked round and saw that Alison was checking the settings on his camera and smiling. He looked back up at his daughter; it was an image that would remain with him through the nightmare to come, an image of such innocence, of such childish beauty, the fun in her touching every corner of her frozen features, that he reached his arms towards her and caught her as she jumped from safety into the greater security of his grasp.

"Get inside now," he said, kissing her ice-cold skin. "We've got enough wood."

"Oh just a while longer, Daddy," she begged, and struggled to free herself from his arms. He let her down and watched her scamper off towards the oak where Willy Crinkleleaf lived. Dominick was there, poking around in the litter that still lay thickly on the ground.

"Stop setting traps for Crinkleleaf!" Brady heard Marianna shout, her shrill voice touched with anger; and Dominick's deeper voice, already breaking, even though he was not yet eleven, replied, "If anything *did* live in the tree it would have been caught by now in my henbane and mandrake snare."

Brady grimaced as he came indoors, and went across to the sink to run hot water onto his frozen hands. "Did you hear that? Henbane, mandrake? The boy's a necromancer. He probably slips us love philtres and listens through the wall."

"Don't be crude," said Alison lightly. "They'd better come in; it's going to snow again."

"Leave them. It's cold, but they're a damn sight better able

to cope with it than I am. I'm going to straighten the tree
out . . ." By which he meant the Christmas tree and its disor-
derly decoration.

He fetched the step-ladder from under the stairs and set it
up against the tree, climbing to the top so that he could rescue
the several yards of tinsel which appeared to have been flung
at random across the lop-sided plastic fairy that surmounted
the giant fir. Dominick appeared in the room, freed of his
winter clothing, and began to hang Christmas cards from the
lengths of twine that Alison had already slung across the barer
parts of the walls. Alison herself sat down by the fire, with a
great basin of chestnuts, and began the laborious task of peel-
ing them, ready to make stuffing for the turkey.

The log fire burned high and hot, and the warmth reached
out and encompassed Brady, giving him a cosy feeling of
being at home, and without worry, and without care . . .

Outside, a brisk winter wind rattled the windows, and sent
the flames in the grate roaring up the chimney.

"What's Marianna up to?" Brady asked, as he laced the
tinsel carefully through the branches of the fir tree.

Dominick didn't answer, and Alison looked up and said to
him. "Dom? Where's Marianna . . .?"

"How should I know?" said Dominick quietly, without
looking up from what he was doing.

Brady felt instantly uncomfortable. Alison was staring at
her son, then she looked round and up at her husband, her
face creasing into a frown of puzzlement. Brady said, "Did
she come in with you?"

"Nope." Dominick sensed that something was wrong; his
whole manner was that of one who knows he should have
exerted more responsibility. He added, "There was a man out
there. She was talking to him . . ."

Alison jumped to her feet. "A man . . .?"

Brady said, "Calm down, Alison. It's probably a neighbour, coming to visit. I'll go and fetch her in . . ."

He stared at Alison, and realized that the two of them were
exchanging a gaze of terror. He frowned. His heart started to
pump with noisy energy. The room swam. Alison stepped
towards him, blood draining from her face. And in that instant, they were aware of it, sensing the danger, sensing the

tragedy. They moved towards each other, but the room had
slipped away, the fire dimmed, the warmth draining away into
a more primal chill. Brady said, "Marianna . . . Oh God . . ."

He heard her call. She was outside the French windows, and
he turned to face her, and saw her standing there, a tiny,
fragile form, all swathed in winter clothing.

"Daddy . . . Daddy, I'm cold . . ."

"Marianna!" he screamed, and began to run towards the
French windows.

With an explosion of glass, and a howl like some supernatural wind, the French doors burst inwards. Marianna's
body was flung at Brady, knocking him down. Above the roar
of wind, he heard three unearthly screams, and recognized
the voices of his family. He tried to see them, to shout their
names, but a dark shape struck him in the face, and a second
figure kicked out at him, taking the breath from his body with
a sickeningly painful blow to his stomach. The lights in the
room, already dim, were extinguished completely. The glow
from the fire, and an eerie glow from the shattered doorway,
were the only light by which Brady could witness the sudden
madness in the room.

The noise abated. There was a muffled crying and the sound
of desperate struggling. Shapes moved all about, dark men in
dark robes, their faces the hideous reflections of animals, a
leering goat, a glitter-eyed hawk, the dull, frightened features
of a cow, the wide grinning features of a frog.

Despite the pain in his body, Brady struggled to his feet,
madness and anger giving him tremendous strength, panic and
fear immunizing him against hurt. He lurched towards one of
the shapes and tore back the hood, screaming, *"Stop this!
Bastards! Bastards!"*

A fat, white face stared at him, the head bald, the eyes tiny
and piggish. The lipless mouth stretched into a quick smile,
while the flared, almost flat nostrils, snorted in breath, a
sound that was not laughter, but was intended to be. The face
was the real face of a man, no mask, but its awful appearance
shocked Brady, and though he reached out to scratch and beat
at the pallid jowls, his blows were tempered.

He felt hands drag him back; he felt blows to his body, then
his arms tied behind his back, manacled; his feet were tied

together, then his thighs; his legs were bent at the knees, and a rope stretched from his neck to his ankles, so that he was trussed like a piece of dead meat. He was lifted and flung against a wall, his nose bursting against the marble edge of the fireplace, and his head cracking, the dull sensation of pain masked by the nausea and muscle-spasm of shock. When he fell to the floor he rolled so that he gazed into the room again, at the whirling, confusing darkness, the men who had attacked him.

Helpless, unable to even cry out, he watched as Alison's naked body was flung between two of the robed figures, then forced to the floor.

"Mark her."

Her arms, locked above her head, showed the strain of muscles almost bursting in their struggle for freedom; a large ball of cloth had been rammed into her mouth, and her head was held quite still as her legs were pulled apart. Brady's heart threatened to burst as he struggled against his bonds, but he could do nothing, and watched the hideous abuse of the woman he so loved with tears in his eyes, and a pain in his belly that threatened to rip him in two.

It seemed to go on forever. Wind howled in through the French windows, and the fire guttered and then dimmed. By its dying light he could see the glistening gold and red object that had been used to "mark" Alison . . . it had the twisted head of an animal, and its shaft was marked with grooves and patterns. The details stayed in Brady's mind almost as powerfully as the shattered, bleeding shape of his wife, who was dragged from his sight.

The Christmas tree fell with a crash, baubles and tinsel scattering across the carpet. The shapes moved about the room, their robes sending wind across Brady's face, their footfalls making the floorboards vibrate with an almost rhythmic pattern.

He saw Marianna, then, her tiny body, clad only in her baggy print dress, arms behind her back, legs locked together, raised in the air. It was a vision of madness, a horrific, incomprehensible sight. Unsupported, she was dangled six feet from the ground, her head almost touching the ceiling. Her eyes streamed tears, her mouth moved as if she were struggling to open it and scream. Her body twisted in the air, and moved, then dropped and bent double, as if unseen hands were passing her between them and had finally flung her across an invisible arm. Folded like a limp rag, her hair covering her face as she twisted in this unseen grasp, she was carried through the French windows and into the frozen night.

A moment later Dom's inert body was carried out by one of the robed figures, then Alison, wrapped in a rug, her hair tied back behind her head so that Brady could see that she was unconscious. As she was carried into the garden her head struck the edge of the door with a sickening thud, a final cruelty to end her torment and violent abuse.

All passion fled from Brady's body; he felt cold on the surface, and ice inside. There was a great clarity in his head, an adrenaline-induced alertness that made him aware of every sound, every murmur, every footfall. He lay quite still, too horrified to really cope with what he had seen, too frightened to move, aware only that he must hear everything that was said.

Three figures stripped the room, taking ornaments, fragments of carpet and chair covering, placing a candle in the middle of the floor and lighting it. Brady smelled something acrid, then something sweet, incense burning, he thought, and giving off an aroma so potent that it could penetrate his blood-filled nostrils. He heard a woman's voice: she was young, she had authority. He saw a man bend towards him, the mask that covered his face that of a pig, its cheeks marked with dark circles, saliva glistening at the mouth. An amulet dangled at the neck: a silver chain, a polished stone head, severed at the neck, the mouth opened in a silent scream.

"He's still alive."

The man's voice was young, unsure; it was sibilant, almost animal. He straightened and moved away. A second shape approached and kicked at Brady, who winced. "He's not wanted." The voice was cold, more experienced. On the dark robes Brady could see the form of a convoluted labyrinth, patterned in dull grey.

"What do we do?"

A pause; a thought; a consideration; then: "Bring the fetch again."

"Are you sure? Is Wickhurst a strong enough source?"

"Then kill him yourself."

"That's forbidden for me."

Irritably: "Then bring the fetch. He's half dead already. Quickly. Magondathog is a long way."

They moved across the room. The words stayed with Brady, the strange words, the sound of the voices, the callous discussion. They moved away, dark shapes in a dark room, extinguishing the candle as they went. They moved away, framed in the doors for a moment, then the sound of them stepping across the garden, their voices a low murmur.

Brady lay in the sudden, unnatural silence. There was no wind. The fire was almost dead, but suddenly embers slipped from the grate and the branches of the fallen tree began to ignite, the flames creeping across that side of the room. He lay staring at the smashed French windows, just able to see the elm trees, outlined against the dark sky. He was still unable to make a sound, although he wanted to scream for help, or with anger, or with agony . . . or with grief.

The broken edges of the door rattled, and glass, strewn across the floor, was kicked aside. But nothing had come in. A moment later Brady cried in his throat as scaly, rough hands gripped him round the neck, half lifting him from the floor as the fingers dug into his windpipe, bending his head back with relentless strength, seeking to snap the bones of his neck. He struggled and twisted, tearing his hands against the rope that secured him, aware of the burning tree and the flames reaching further into the room. His eyes bulged, his mouth, sewn tight with thread, he thought, stretched until he thought his lips would tear; he snorted blood and mucus into his lungs, and began to drown on his own wounds. The fingers pressed harder and his body was shaken from side to side. He thought his eyes would burst, the pain in them, and the colour, and then the darkness as the pressure built up.

Death came quickly, then, consciousness ebbing away as his body starved of oxygen, the bones in his neck cracking. The last thing he knew was that he slipped from his body and looked down upon it, and saw it lying there, all broken and twisted, its eyes bulging like billiard balls, the skin flushed red, the fingers tied by no rope that he could see, wriggling in a last, frantic attempt to free themselves.

A shape bent over this body, its black hands squeezing and squeezing, its monstrous back arched with effort. He couldn't see the face of the creature, and could only glimpse it as an intangible presence above his corpse. But as he floated away, as he abandoned his body to death, he reached down and began to scrabble at the gigantic fists that were closing around the dying man.

— THREE

THE BEST PART of the night, and yet in many ways the worst part, was that time between two and five in the morning. Almost as if they were responding to a signal, the patients on King George Ward fell silent at about two a.m., their coughing, muttering, snoring and general restlessness fading away into an occasional murmur, and the faintest of wheezes.

On a good night—and most nights were good—there was nothing for the on-duty nurse to do save check each bed once an hour, and sit at the desk, in the light of a single lamp, and read, or write letters, or study for exams. On those rare nights were one patient needed constant supervision, the nights passed rapidly.

Nurse Mai-li Baker much preferred a night without complications, but she had great difficulty in keeping awake when she read, or tried to write, and it was those restful three hours that caused her the most problems.

To remain alert she settled into a routine; a walk round the ward every half an hour, followed by fifteen minutes reading, a glass of milk, or cup of coffee, then a brisk check through the toilets, wash-rooms and supply rooms. She was only twenty-one, a small girl with her mother's Chinese features strongly represented in her face, and in the brisk, slightly curve-legged way she walked. Her father was dead, had died at sea, in fact, not far from the colonial island off the coast of Mainland China where he and Mai-li's mother had met.

Mai-li, the sole offspring of that short marriage, had never known her homeland. She was quite English to talk to, to listen to, and in her likes and loves; English, in fact, in everything but looks.

She was an attractive, quite shy girl, and very popular with medical students and male nurses. If she used the silence of the dead hours of morning for any sort of critical thought it was to consider her various suitors, to try and decide which would be her best course of action in the matter of her heart, and in the direction of her affection.

At three in the morning she interrupted her idle contemplation of the young, slightly aristocratic medical student, Paul Boyd (who was, perhaps, the keenest of the students on her at the moment) to make her routine check around the ward. As she passed the rest-room she stepped inside and switched on the kettle. It would be nicely boiled by the time she had completed her round.

King George Ward contained sixty beds, arranged in small rooms of four or six, each room open to the corridor. The corridor ran in a square with the utility rooms in the middle. The intensive care patients, or those who needed special medication on a regular basis, were grouped in four open bays opposite the nursing station where the night nurse would sit. Ten private rooms were grouped on the right of the station; a lounge area, in which visitors and patients could meet more comfortably than by the bedside, stretched away to the left.

Mai-li paced round the corridor, stepping into each small room in turn and looking at each patient just long enough to establish that they were peacefully asleep. When she reached the ten private rooms she simply peered through the door, checked the system of lights above the beds, and ascertained that there was nothing more than peaceful slumber occurring within the cell. She opened the door to Mr. Arthur and checked the drip feed that stood by his bed. He was a very old man, quite strong in spirit, but was still unable to take solid food after an operation upon his stomach. In the next room was the young car crash victim, John Spencer, his head still bandaged, his limbs in plaster. He was well recovered from the accident, but given to fits of screaming in the middle of the night. No audio link was necessary to the nursing station; his yelling was always clearly audible.

There were two appendicitis recoveries, private patients, both business men of sorts. They had little time for the ordinary niceties, preferring to be woken at five and provided with the financial papers which they studiously read through most of the day. They were unaware of each other's existence; the nursing staff had nicknamed them tweedledee and tweedledum; the names were quite appropriate, since both men showed the obvious trouser belt strain of too many business lunches.

In room number six was Mister Mystery.

Nurse Baker stared through the window at the peacefully sleeping man. He lay on his back, his arms outside the covers, a drip-feed in place. She could just make out the rise and fall of his chest.

She opened the door and crept inside, lifted the man's wrist and felt his pulse. Leaning over she raised his eyelid slightly and checked his pupil response by the light of a small pen torch. She placed the arm back down and shone the torch onto the stubby face.

By looking hard, she could just make out the remnants of the bruising on his throat and face. His body had fought long and hard to repair the damage to his tissue and bones, but the battle was nearly won. The battle for his mind was another matter.

Mai-li had heard stories about the man's arrival. He had been in a coma, the same coma that imprisoned his reason at the moment. By rights, she had been told, he should have been dead: his windpipe had been crushed, the neck bones cracked and splintered, and on the verge of severing the spinal cord. His throat, face and shoulders had been black and blue with bruising. He had bled into his lungs from the nasal mucosa, and from perforations of his peritoneal cavity caused by splinters from his fractured ribs.

The man's injuries were concomitant with a crash, with being crushed or having fallen . . . all save the bruising on the neck. It was still possible to see the marks of the huge fingers that had caused that!

Strangled, beaten, crushed . . . left for dead. He had been found in the badly burned lounge of his house. The flames had been doused by the hidden sprinkler system in the walls, otherwise—Mai-li had heard—the house would have burned to the ground, and the evidence of the brutal assault (obviously intended to be a murder) with it.

Some inner strengh, some awesome power of spirit, or of soul, had kept the man alive. When he had been brought to the hospital his hands and feet were locked together as if they had been tied. The skin of his wrists and ankles showed the marks of a thin cord, but no cord had bound him, even though his body continued to believe itself tied.

Over the first weeks that rigid posture had relaxed. He had been fed intravenously, massaged daily, exercised and encouraged to return to consciousness, even as his bones were healed, and his neck operated upon to reduce the danger of his vertebrae snapping through completely. When Mai-li Baker had taken up her position on King George Ward, the man called Daniel Brady was simply known as an enigma, a man to be washed, cleaned, turned, exercised, spoken to, and checked every hour on the hour for the slightest sign of a return to consciousness.

Tonight, two months after he had been brought into the hospital, there was no change whatsoever in his condition, a fact that the nurse noted quickly on the chart at the end of the bed. As she pocketed her pen, however, she stopped, sniffed, and sniffed again. It was there, stronger than before. A smell like burning wood, but scented wood; a very strange odour that might well have been drifting in from outside the hospital . . . except that she never noticed it anywhere but in this one room.

With a quick glance round to satisfy herself that nothing was burning, Nurse Baker left the room, haunted by that tenuous aromatic, recognizing something about it, yet not really recognizing it at all.

She finished her round and went to the tiny kitchen area, where her kettle had boiled, gone off the boil, and needed a little re-heating. It was as she heaped coffee into her personal mug that she heard the swing doors at the Victoria end of King George Ward open and shut again, then bang open three times, very noisily.

All blood drained from her face and she felt her legs go

weak. She edged to the corridor and peered round at the distant doors. They were still moving slightly, as if in a wind. A moment later she heard the doors at the other end of the ward, where King George opened into the general stairwell, slammed back against the wall, and repeatedly pushed. This was the second night running that this had happened. A patient, obviously from one of the other wards, had a very peculiar idea of practical joking. The previous evening she had heard the man —if man it was—running quickly away from the Victoria Ward exit, and had followed him for a few yards, but had not caught sight of him.

She walked up to the swing doors and peered through the glass, but the stairwell was deserted, dimly illuminated by a single yellow lamp above. As she stood there, once again she smelled that strange pungency, less scented than before, sharper, bitter. It was just a hint, like the fleeting smell of burning incense caught outside a church.

Nurse Baker walked slowly back along the corridor, peering into the private rooms, lingering outside Brady's room, and staring at the motionless man inside. Some thought nagged at her, some connection or subdued awareness, that she couldn't bring to the fore.

Slowly she returned to her station, opposite the open bays of intensive care and special treatment patients. One of them was restless, making quiet, but disturbed sounds in his throat. For a second she couldn't identify, in the subdued light, who it was. As she recognized Mister Henderson, recovering from heart surgery and only regaining his strength slowly, she took a step towards him, checking the time on her watch.

And something ice cold, like a tremendous gust of wind, swept past her, blowing her hair and clothes, and rattling the privacy curtains on their metal rails. The bed nearest to the nurse rolled away from the wall, and turned sharply in the centre of the room, the drip feed attached to its occupant crashing to the floor. The man in the bed sat up blearily, realized what was happening and yelled; his yell turned to a scream, and Nurse Baker ran towards him as he was tipped from the bed and apparently dragged across the floor, to be flung heavily against the window, which shattered spectacularly. The man's body vanished, leaving tatters of pyjama and flesh on the jagged edges of the window.

The nurse shrieked and ran from the station, towards the small kitchen area. Her mind was spinning, she was shocked, terrified, and utterly confused. Confused, that is, save for one thing; whatever was happening was related to the mystery man, Brady. It was Brady. She *had* to tell someone.

She picked up a blunt-edged bread knife and stared around at the rest of the kitchen area. She had no real idea what to do, except to run for help. The noise in the intensive care bay was loud, patients shouting, talking, calling for her.

Clutching the knife in her hand—for what reason she had no idea, she just knew it felt good—she began to walk back towards the station.

She had just reached the door when a sheet of glass from the broken window swept towards her, slashing across her throat in two rapid, powerful motions. She was knocked back against the wall, her eyes staring with that shock that immediately precedes death. With the third massive strike from the invisibly wielded fragment of glass those eyes rolled up into their sockets, staring white and blind as the blood-drenched head bounced yards along the corridor.

─*FOUR*───────────

HE CAME UP from the blackness, eyes opening and focusing on the ventilation grill in the ceiling.

Three times before, his mind had gathered strength and pushed aside the shadows, rising towards consciousness through the chaotic images of fear, anger and despair. Three times the ghosts of that night just before Christmas had risen and begun to scream, the power of their emotion overwhelming and subduing the return to consciousness.

Had anyone been watching, on those three occasions, they might have seen the man's motionless hands clench and then relax, his body twitch slightly, his head turn from right to left. A murmur in the throat would have given the lie to the explosive scream that had resounded through the drugged space of his brain.

The time had not been right. The body was too weak and it drained strength from the mind.

Now the body was strong again, and this time the return to consciousness was successful. The shadows parted. The darkness of night gave way to the colours of dawn, and a waking dream that hovered on the edge of nightmare, images and events that seemed to be waiting for the eyes to open . . .

He saw the white ceiling; the shadowy edge of a light; a tube of colourless liquid attached to a deflating plastic bag . . .

Waiting for the ears to begin to register sound . . .

The clatter of a trolley, piled high with the empty dishes

*from breakfast; voices; someone calling, someone shouting in-
structions . . .*

Waiting for the skin to start to respond to sensation . . .

*Crisp, hard sheets below the hands; tickling, irritating sen-
sation on the right arm where the drip connected; warmth on
the skin; soreness on the back . . .*

Waiting for the nose to become aware of odours . . .

*The peculiar hospital smell of ether, disinfectant; the faint
perfume of flowers; the distant, just-hinted odour of faeces; a
pungent, strange smell of burned wood, or herbs . . .*

Waiting for the mind to remember . . .

*An explosion of glass! Darkness! Cold! The glitter of ani-
mal eyes; the stench of their breath! Alison, held to the floor
struggling, and little Marianna, her body lifted into the air,
and Dominick, carried away! The dark confusion and the terrible screaming of a woman attacked in the most brutal way!
And . . .*

Came awake!

Sat up in bed and screamed at the top of his voice!

The room shook and swam with images. Alison ran towards
him, vanished; Marianna screamed from behind and he
twisted in the bed, jerking the needle from his arm so that
glucose and blood flowed onto the sheets. Dominick fled into
the shadows, pursued by a robed figure that raised a jewelled
sword and struck down at him.

And Brady screamed, his eyes screwed shut again, his face
flushed with heat and anger and agony. The sinews of his neck
stood out like great ridges of rock; muscles burst, skin split,
bones crushed together in his neck as he flung back his head
and cried with every ounce of energy in his body, every tiny air
space of his lungs. The volume of the cry became a wind, a
harrowing gale of terror . . . and sadness.

By the time two members of the nursing staff arrived, Brady
was racking with sobs, bleeding from his mouth, and beginning to bruise where the effect of tension had ruptured his
tissues. He was forced back down to a lying position, but he
fought the nurses, crying, "Alison! Alison! The bastards are
killing her. Alison! My daughter . . . my daughter Mari, Dom
. . . they're killing them! Let me go, let me go!"

He flung the nurses back and staggered from the bed, but

his legs, white and shakey after so long without use, refused to take his weight, and he collapsed heavily, still screaming the names of his family. He was helped back to bed. His mouth was foam flecked, and the foam was shaded with red.

At last a needle slipped into his arm, and a calming drug coursed through his veins, reducing the muscular tension in his body, and the terrible confusion in his mind.

In the half-light of that dreamy, drug-controlled state there were other images; remembered images from the three months of coma, images seen, perhaps, through his closed lids, or sensed by his mind, or seen during brief seconds when his eyes opened and closed again. There were the anonymous faces of doctors and nurses, pale and intense, bland and mostly bored. There was a face he knew to be his brother-in-law Bill, peering down at him and shaking his head. Others, friends perhaps, colleagues, all staring at him, all expressing bemusement in their pallid features.

And there was one face in particular, unfamiliar to him, a face that bent close, that was accompanied by a strange smell, the smell of burning. It was a woman's face. She was pretty, though her hair was unkempt. Her breath had an odour of garlic to it, in this half-remembered dream. She stared at him and stroked him; she whispered to him, and touched a strange smelling unguent to his face and neck. Perhaps he had dreamed her. Perhaps it was just another nurse.

The face faded. The drugs faded. Memory of Alison and Marianna and Dominick returned, and with it a renewed burst of hysterical anger. The anger was furious and uncontrollable; he tore at the bed clothes, tore at the curtains on the windows, smashed glass and trays to the ground, and beat wildly but helplessly at the nursing staff who sedated him.

Then there was sadness. Uncontrollable weeping. He wept as food was helped into his mouth; he wept when he was washed; he cried Marianna's name through the racking sobs of a most awesome loneliness. He remembered her standing on the woodshed, all tiny and fragile, a doll with two gaps in her teeth and that impish grin; eyes twinkling behind tiny round spectacles; feet, clad in immense red wellington boots, kicking off from the woodshed as she launched into his arms and snuggled to his breast.

Marianna!

And, in his more rational moments, there were the questions. Who had they been? And why had they attacked the Bradys? And why had they taken only the three of them, and left Brady himself for dead? What on earth—or in hell—had attacked him? Why them, why that one family?

Who had they been? Where had they come from?

Slowly the flooding sadness subsided, leaving a great, gouging ache in his breast, but no longer causing his mind to suffer the turmoil of madness. Other emotions began to make themselves felt: bitterness; and hate. Hate for those who had done this thing to him, terrible hate for their arrogance in invading his home, and his life, for their brutality, for their unspeakable crime.

— *FIVE* ———————————————

THE DAY AFTER he had regained consciousness, Daniel Brady received his first visitor. Brady was mildly sedated, and in a melancholy frame of mind, the fear, the hatred and the intense bitterness pushed down by drugs. He sat, propped up in bed, staring out of the window.

The door to his private room was opened by a petite blonde nurse who said softly, "The police are here. Do you feel up to it?"

Brady turned his head to look at her. "How many of them?"

"Just one. He's been here on and off for the last three months. I think he'll be able to tell you . . . you know, something about . . . well, that night."

"Send him in," said Brady, easing himself a little more upright. He had felt a shiver of black anger as the girl had referred to "that night." He knew it as just a matter of hours before the phantom that he was suppressing came screaming out of the darkness again.

Superintendent Andrew Sutherland was a tall, overweight man, with a ruddy face, and receding grey hair, combed back slick against his skull. He smiled broadly at Brady as he dragged up a chair next to the bed. He opened his tan raincoat, but didn't take it off. Brady thought that he might sit across the chair, leaning on its back, but the man sat properly, almost primly, legs crossed, hands folded neatly in his lap.

"How are you feeling, Mister Brady? Or is that question as cruel as it is silly?"

Brady tried to smile. The policeman's eyes were as grey as his hair, islands of pallid, unfocussed strength in the pudgy pink jowls. He looked like a country policeman but with the icy-eyed good looks of an actor.

"I'm very weak. I'm very confused. I'm growing more bitter all the time. I can't get my daughter's face out of my mind. They haunt me, all of them haunt me. I'm telling you, Superintendent, I shan't sleep, nor rest, until I avenge Alison for what happened to her; I want those men killed. I will kill them myself."

The superintendent chose to ignore that last statement. He said, instead, "You know then. You've been told . . ."

Brady looked away. "That they've disappeared? That they were taken without trace? I didn't need to be told. I think I knew when they took them; I think I knew while I was in a coma; I certainly knew when I came out of it." He turned back to Sutherland. "What else can you tell me?"

Sutherland pursed his lips as he stared at the sedated man. "Your brother-in-law, one William Suchock, found you . . ."

"I know my brother-in-law's name."

"Sorry Mister Brady, force of habit. Mister Suchock found you on the same evening of the attack. You were as good as dead. The room had been burned, the Christmas tree, the carpets, the curtains, some furniture ruined; but you have an efficient sprinkler system which doused the fire before it could do any real damage."

Brady nodded his head, not for any reason except that within himself he was recognizing the advantage of farsightedness. In the months after he and his family had moved into Brook's Corner, Marianna had taken to sleep-walking, and ending up at the fire place, trying to light the fire with matches, or burning tapers from the gas stove. The reason for her strange, somnambulistic mission had defeated them, but the worry had been there that she might cause a fire. The sprinkler system had cost very little to install, and was an added security.

Sutherland went on. "He called an ambulance at once, and he called the police. You were as good as dead. You had been strangled, and your ribs crushed. It's something of a mystery —not to mention a miracle—that you're actually still alive. In fact, for a few minutes it's quite possible that you weren't . . ."

Frowning, Brady said, "I don't understand."

"You will," said Sutherland. "Your brother-in-law will explain. I need to talk to you about more important things. The fact is, you *are* alive, and you've remained mentally alert after a most vicious, brutal and callous attack. Your family are missing. I have to tell you, with some regret, that they are missing without trace. We have done everything possible to find them, assured by Mister Suchock that they were in the house with you earlier that evening, and that they had no plans to go away. Airports, sea-ports, all were alerted. Our divisions throughout the country were given photographs of the three of them. We checked the roads, and country around your house across an area of several miles. We've contacted every one of your family, and friends, although we may have missed a few friends. Nothing . . ."

"Nothing at all?"

"Not a trace. I'm very sorry, Mister Brady. I must also tell you that this is the third such incident we have heard of in the past year. It's essential we hear from you what happened, and what you remember."

The third such incident! The words echoed in Brady's mind. It added, strangely, a sense of insult to his most horrifying injury. The animals that had attacked his family had attacked before, and twice before had got away with it! Not just Alison, Marianna and Dominick, but others, other innocent people, abused, defiled, perhaps killed, stolen . . .

"Bastards . . ." he said and repeated with as much vehemence as his weakened, subdued body could muster, *"Bastards!"*

"Tell me what you remember about them."

Sutherland's unflustered tone induced calm in Brady, who said, "There were five or six. Hard to tell, they struck me down almost at once. One was a woman, youngish, chubby; she . . ." the words stuck in his throat and he felt tears rush to his eyes; but he blinked them back, swallowed the sour taste of vomit in his mouth, and said, "She raped . . . Alison. A sort of gold phallic object. Horrible. Why? Why would they do that? Why not just take her, why subject her to such a foul abuse?'' He choked back the sudden anger, saying, ''Oh my God! I must find them, I must find them . . .''

But he had started to become agitated, twisting in the bed, and struggling to sit up. Sutherland rose from his seat, pressured his shoulders and eased him back, uttering soothing words. A nurse came in, frowned, felt Brady's forehead. ''Will you be much longer? He really should rest.''

''I'm alright,'' said Brady, feeling gradually calmer. ''I want to get this over with.''

The nurse remained in the room. Sutherland sat down on his chair again, and prompted, ''A woman.''

''She seemed to be the leader. They wore dark robes, and animal masks; they might have been real animal faces. One . . . he was fat, short, looked mongoloid. I shan't forget that face, like a grinning toad, but white, grey white, like death, like a corpse.''

''What else?''

''The others . . . just voices. Men, youngish sounding. One wore an amulet, like a severed head. Stone, or dull metal. One had a pattern on his robe, like the classic labyrinth, the pattern of turf mazes . . .''

''Could you sketch that amulet if we asked you to?''

''I could try.''

''Can you remember any dialogue? Any words, any strange words?''

Brady thought hard. The event was so confusing, and tinged with such pain in his mind, that little coherent memory came through.

''Wickhurst. Something like that. 'Is Wickhurst powerful enough' someone said.''

Sutherland wrote down the word. ''That's useful. Anything else?''

''One of them was forbidden to kill.''

Something else . . . but he couldn't place it, couldn't remember.

Sutherland said, ''One of them obviously wasn't. Although he didn't reckon on a man of your physical stamina. What time did they come?''

Brady didn't know. "Early evening. Marianna was outside.
It was dark, maybe seven o'clock. Marianna . . ." As he said
the name he turned back to stare at Sutherland, who was
watching him with both compassion and interest. In Brady's
mind was a peculiar image. "She was lifted in the air. I
couldn't see who was holding her. Lifted . . . spun around. I
couldn't see how . . ."

Sutherland scribbled frantically in his small notebook. Then
he turned back a few pages and looked up at Brady. "Do any
of these words mean anything to you? Antherrogatha."

Brady shook his head. Sutherland said, "Baelenneas."

"Not a thing."

"Magondathog . . ."

Brady turned sharply. The word, meaningless in itself, set
bells ringing in his head. Yes, that word, that strange word, he
had heard it twice as he had lain, tied and beaten in the darkness. He said so, adding, "A place name, I think. What does it
mean?"

"I wish we knew."

"And the others? The other words?"

Sutherland smiled. "*I* made those up. But the word Magondathog has been reported, now, in all three attacks. Part of it
may be the old Celtic word for 'stone.' The rest is, I was told,
etymological nonsense. Whatever that is." Sutherland rose
from the chair, reached out to tug the blanket up around
Brady's chest. He looked at the man for a moment, then
smiled thinly. "I really am terribly sorry, Mister Brady. I can
understand your anger. God knows, I can understand that. I
would ask you only to come to me the *moment* you feel you
need someone to turn to, to talk to, to talk you out of an action that might be regarded as criminal, justifiable though it
might be. This is a bizarre and baffling incident, and like you
yourself I don't intend to ever let it slip down my list of
priorities."

"Thank you," said Brady weakly.

"Oh. One other thing . . . you work at the Ministry of
Defence at Hillingvale?"

"Yes I do."

"Your work is classified, so I'm not going to ask you to talk
about it. But I've obtained a release from your department

and have read through the notes on your project. I don't pretend to understand it, all that Electromagnetic transmission, extra-sensory pick up. It sounds to me like you were working on what I call the paranormal. So my question is a simple one: could you have released something . . . something unusual, something not physical like you or I, but more . . . metaphysical? Could your work be involved in what happened to you?"

Brady stared up at the policeman, horrified at the suggestion, remembering that last day in the lab, and the strange event that had occurred there. He said, "I don't think so. I can't imagine how, or what." He didn't go on to voice his thought that somehow, just somehow, it might have been possible for him to have *attracted* something to the site of his work.

It was a chilling thought. It was a terrifying thought.

Bill Suchock didn't look at all like the highly qualified draftsman he was; rather, he looked like a highly paid builder, the sort of man that can lend his hand to anything, be it bricklaying, carpentry or road-laying. He was short and stocky, his hair receding and slicked back; he wore donkey-jackets by preference, and dusty overalls. But the thick fingers and chubby hands that could turn themselves so well to the hard graft of do-it-yourself, were also capable of fine drawing, and exercising a finesse with the delicate pens of his trade that was the envy of his colleagues.

He got on well with Dan Brady, though their interests were considerably apart, and he didn't pretend to understand, or like, that part of Brady's work which the Ministry of Defence man was permitted to talk about. But they shared an interest in family, in sport, and in long trips around England. Bill Suchock didn't find it necessary to always engage in deep conversation with his brother-in-law, and Dan Brady, for his part, seemed quite content to enjoy the ease with which the two men could co-exist in each other's company.

The thorn in the side of the ease of all relationships connected with the Suchocks and the Bradys was Rosemary Suchock, Brady's younger sister. She was devoted to her husband and her child, clinging to them as if her life depended on them, which in more than one way it did. She was intolerably

and appallingly jealous of her brother's success, and the accu-
mulation of material things around him. This jealousy manifested itself in tantrums, comparisons and, most insidious of
all, an acute and abrasive criticism.

And yet it was Rosemary's voice which raised the loudest in
favour of family Christmasses, inviting their sturdy, widowed
father to join the fun from his home in Durham. And if she
was aggressively self-centered about her own child—a trait
that was beginning to have its effect upon him—she was never
less than loving to her brother's kids, and never less than
generous.

She was beautiful, slim, and almost always on edge. She
would have done anything for her father, to make his last
years comfortable, and no matter how much she irritated him,
Dan Brady couldn't help loving her.

And that, of course, is what she wanted. Put in the simplest
terms—and there were no terms simpler than those expressed
by Brady and Bill Suchock during their quiet drinks together
when they played at psychoanalysts—Rosemary needed to
love and be loved, and the importance of love in her adult life
was a making-up for the greater attention that Dan himself
had received as a child.

That's all it was. The problem stated. And the answer im-
plied: Keep the woman feeling wanted. And the next drink's
on you.

Poor Rosemary.

She had been devastated by the discovery of Dan's near
murder and the loss of his family. Like a hen without a head
she had rushed around desperate to help, knowing that she
could help, made useless by her own grief and confusion. Bill
had kept a clear head. He had assisted the police, had visited
the hospital almost daily to see his brother-in-law, and had
talked to the comatose Dan for hours, hoping that the words
would penetrate the unconscious levels of the mind, to the
alert man he believed to be trapped within. Nevertheless,
Rosemary put her weight into the task of tidying and redecor-
ating Dan's lounge, ready for when the family was brought
together again.

And the fear had happened.

•   •   •

There was a presence in the house, a residuum of evil; they could feel it towards dusk. It seemed to ooze out of the stone walls of Brook's Corner, and gather in the lounge where they were working. It lowered the fire, lowered the temperature in the room; it rattled the French windows, blew cold and icy in the faces of the nervous couple.

"Let's go, Bill. Let's get out of here." Rosemary was standing by the door, arms folded, looking pale and very frightened.

The windows of the lounge had been repaired, the carpets replaced, and Bill had fetched a second-hand suite from friends of his. Rosemary had spent the day covering them. Bill had worked on painting where the gloss had been scorched on the doors and windows.

"Something doesn't want us here," she said. "Bill, I'm frightened—"

"You're imagining things," he said. "It's the wind, and your nerves. There's nothing here."

As darkness came down outside, Rosemary put on the lights. The wind guttered down the chimney. Upstairs, a door banged loudly. Rosemary began to feel so on edge that she wanted to scream, to run from the house and never come back . . .

She turned to Bill. "For God's sake, let's call it a day!"

And the lights in the lounge exploded!

Rosemary screamed. The room was plunged into sudden, terrifying darkness, and the wind blowing through the chimney dulled the fire until the coals barely glowed.

The French windows were flung open: Bill's pot of paint was sent flying, spilling onto some newspapers.

The two of them grabbed their coats and fled from the house.

The next day Bill went back, cleaned up the mess and finished the painting. He went during the day, and stayed only two hours.

Thereafter, his visits were increasingly brief.

When the call from the hospital came, that Brady was conscious, the Suchocks were in Durham visiting Brady's father. Rosemary decided to stay on for a day or two, as was the original plan, because her father was ill, and needed caring for and feeding. When he was better, the two of them would travel down to see Dan.

Bill Suchock took the Intercity to London, early in the morning, the day after Dan's recovery. He took a commuter train to Iver, a taxi home, and picked up his own car. From there, equipped with fruit, and photographs of the refurbished lounge, he made his grim way to the hospital. No matter how cheerful he tried to be, he couldn't conquer the terrible dread that pounded in his chest: did Dan know yet? Did he know that Alison and the family had disappeared without trace? If the police had been to see him, then yes, perhaps he did. Perhaps the nursing staff had told him. But perhaps it was being left to Bill, as a member of the family, to break the tragic news. It was a responsibility he accepted, and was geared up towards; it didn't stop him feeling sick with nerves.

"Hello Dan."

Dan Brady looked round from the window, stared at his brother-in-law, then gave the merest, weariest of smiles. "Bill . . ." he acknowledged; then turned away.

"I can't say you look like the sunshine's coming out of you. I'm not surprised." Nervously, Suchock took a seat, placed the grapes by the bed and undid his jacket. He had been instantly taken aback by Brady's appearance. Used to seeing a pale-faced, supine, sleeping man, this sudden redness of face, the wild dishevelment of the hair, the drawn features, and dark rimmed, sunken, angry eyes gave Brady the look of a fiend.

Brady said, "I know about Alison. And the kids. I'm going to find them, Bill. I'm going to find them, and I'm going to hunt down those bastards and break every bone . . ." his voice had begun to rise. He caught himself short, turned slightly, then glanced at Suchock. "I'm under sedation. By rights I ought to be flat on my back, but this is what anger does, Bill. It keeps me walking, keeps me thinking. When the drugs wear off . . . God knows what will happen. I dread to think. But it's got to come. I want it to come. I'm going to kill them. I've got to get them back, I've got to find Alison." Tears welled slightly in the haunted eyes. "I can't live without those kids, Bill. I need them more than . . ."

"Hey, take it easy. Come and sit down and talk to me." Bill rose and for the first time embraced his friend. Brady's voice wavered between the fatigued and the hysterical; he was rambling, and Suchock wasn't sure quite who Brady would kill, and who he would find, although he rightly assumed a reference to the person, or persons, who had kidnapped his family.

"Where's Rosemary?"

"In Durham, looking after your father. They'll both be down in a day or two."

Brady nodded. Seated on the edge of his bed, he stared at Suchock, who grew uncomfortable beneath the gaze. He looked tired, he knew, and unshaven. He needed a cigarette badly, but rules were rules . . .

Quickly, then, reducing the horror to a minimum, Brady told his brother-in-law about the evening, about what had happened. Suchock's face paled. Even in so muted an account, the details were horrific. He winced and shook his head as Brady mentioned Alison's rape. "Bastards . . . who could do such a thing . . . bastards . . ."

"I've seen films about Satanists. Or gangs of kids who invade homes."

"*Clockwork Orange* . . . disgusting."

"But there was something about this group. Something different. I felt it from *before* they came into the house. I felt the evil. Whatever they were, Christ they were organized. Something terrible, Bill. Something truly evil: gathering . . ."

Suchock frowned. "Gathering?"

"That's the sense I got. They were gathering. They took my kids as part of it, but they didn't need me, so they tried to kill me . . ."

Appalled silence. Suchock said. "The police . . ."

Shaking his head, smiling almost cynically, Brady said, "They know nothing. Although it's happened before. I told them what I remembered, they told me what they knew." He stared at Suchock. "How about you, Bill? You found me. Tell me what happened."

"The odd thing is," said Suchock carefully, leaning back in the uncomfortable hospital chair, "I reckon you died briefly. I reckon you really did. I came round for a quick, pre-Christ-

mas drink, mainly because Rosemary was being a little diffi-
cult, and I needed some air, and a Scotch."

"What time did you come?"

"About ten o'clock. The house was in darkness, which is
unusual for your place. No answer from the front. Smell of
burning, which got me agitated, so I went round the side and
came in through what was left of your French windows. The
fire was out by then. You were on the floor trussed up like a
bag of beans. Except that you weren't."

Brady frowned.

"No ropes, no cord, nothing, but I couldn't get your arms
apart, or your legs. You were barely breathing. I called for
help at once."

"Why did you think I was dead?"

"I saw your ghost. That's all it could have been . . . if we
rule out imagination, and we both know I've got none of that.
As I came round the side of the house I swear I saw you standing in the windows; then you backed away into the room. I
swear it, Dan. And your face wasn't black and grey with bruising, which it was when I found you. Your spirit, something
like that, and when I found you, more dead than alive, I
reckoned you'd probably slipped away for a moment, just a
moment, and the sound of my voice brought you back. That's
why I came in here whenever I could and talked to you. In case
it brought you back."

Brady smiled. "Thanks Bill. I remember more of those
whispered talks than you'd think possible. I remember a lot
from being in a coma."

*A face, female . . . staring down at him . . . young, pretty,
dishevelled, the smell of sweet herbs burning . . .*

"What was that?"

"What was what?"

"That look. A faraway look. You were thinking of something . . ."

"A girl. She visited me here several times. I didn't know
her."

"A nurse, probably." Brady shook his head. Suchock sug-
gested, "Someone from Hillingvale?"

"Perhaps. It's odd, though. There's a smell in this room,
too. Like burning, like a sort of incense . . ."

"I've noticed it frequently. So have the nursing staff."

Brady stared at the other man for a moment, trying to mentally articulate the other thing that had been worrying him. It was to do with the nursing staff, something about their attitude to him, their behaviour towards him. He said, "Do I frighten the nurses on this ward? I ask because they behave oddly. Nothing I can put my finger on, just a feeling that they'd be happier not coming into the room . . ."

Suchock stood up and walked to the window, to peer out across the fields of Berkshire, and the distant town. "Truth is, Dan, they think you're haunted. They *are* afraid, but it's the sort of fear that people get through rumour, rather than fact."

"They think I'm haunted?"

"Two nurses, and one patient, have been very horribly killed in the last three months. One poor girl was decapitated; the other thrown down the stairwell, which from here is six concrete floors. The patient jumped, or was thrown, through a plate-glass window . . . a window that is supposed to be unbreakable with ordinary human strength."

Brady turned, wincing a little as the bones in his neck gave him pain. He was not fully right, although it was only violent movement that showed him the weaknesses still residual in his body. "That's horrible. But why should they be . . . what I mean is . . . why me?"

"Nothing more than the fact that you came here as an enigma, a man treated cruelly, with an inexplicable disappearance associated with you. You're not someone who came in here for heart surgery, or a peptic ulcer. You came out of the dark, and remained in that dark for three months. You come; a nurse is killed, then a second nurse, and a patient; there's poltergeist activity on the wards, the sound of running . . . and a smell like burning, which is always present in two places: at the entrance to the ward. . . and in your room." Suchock turned back from the window and picked up his coat. "You've received the best medical attention, believe me. No one's shirked on that. I made sure of it. But don't blame the staff for being a little apprehensive. This is a haunted ward . . . and you're a haunted man. What worries me, Dan . . ." he hesitated. Should he say the thought that nagged at him?

Brady said it for him. "You're worried that there might be

something in it, that I am—somehow—the cause . . .''

Bill Suchock just shrugged, then reached out to shake Brady's hand. "I've got to go, Dan. Rosemary and the Old Man will call by in a couple of days. I'll be by tomorrow. And you'll be out in a week, anyway."

"Thanks for coming, Bill. I appreciate it. I appreciate everything. Please keep coming . . . no matter what happens to me."

Suchock glanced at him nervously, then smiled. "You're family, Dan. You're family."

—*Six*——————————————

A FEW MINUTES before the official breaking of dawn, a car
drew up silently on the far side of the road to Brook's Corner.
It was an S-registered Cortina, painted black; the windows
were dark too, allowing the occupant to observe without being
observed, even though the car's morbid appearance would attract attention.

Headlights extinguished, the car remained still and quiet,
cooling in the crisp, frost-touched atmosphere. It was beginning to grow light, and the house at Brook's Corner could be
seen through the beech trees as a tall, dark shape against a
sombre grey sky.

Jack Baron valued these quiet, haunted moments at the
beginning of a new day. He stepped from his car and closed
the door very carefully. The nearest house to Brook's Corner
was three hundred yards away, but he wanted no dogs barking
at the sound of his car-door slamming. Any time that he felt a
house-check was in order he would opt for the dawn patrol.
Even dogs were sleepy at this time, and the occupants of a
house, almost certainly in bed, would be so deeply enslum-
bered that he could safely walk through their property with the
impertinence that his job required.

He had no such worries with Brook's Corner. He knew that
the occupants were elsewhere. Force of habit had made him
arrive so early . . . that and the fact that the police *did* regularly check the property, and the brother-in-law—Suchock

57

—was forever pottering about, painting or replastering.

Baron was in his late thirties, a man of medium build and medium height, but tough to look at, and tough in his attitude and behaviour. He was an East-Ender, a cockney born and bred, and enough of his life had been street-life for him to be able to use his fists, and yet hold the police in healthy respect. Dressed in a leather jacket and tight, faded denims, he ran quickly across the road and in through the gate of the house. He wanted a cigarette, but made do with a reassuring touch on the bulky packet in his breast pocket. He checked the frontage of the house from a distance, then walked more confidently along the curving driveway, heading for the side of the house where there were French windows that he could easily open.

This was the second time Baron had undertaken this routine; his second visit.

The first, prompted by a message from a certain client of his, had been made shortly after the fire, nearly three months ago. It had been an unsatisfactory search, since the police had still been showing an active interest in the events that had occurred here, and he had been interrupted in his work by their untimely arrival.

He had had other clients to worry about, and the strange woman had only been giving him a tip-off anyway, a suggestion as to how he might piece together extra facts in his search for her husband. Baron was a moderately able private investigator, but was most able when it came to sniffing out men of his own class, criminals who might have welched on a deal, or informed on a gang. At the tracing of dissident ganglanders he was second to none; at tracking down errant husbands he was as good as he needed to be; but the crazy American woman, who would only deal with him indirectly, had given him a case that was totally beyond his ability.

He had got nowhere in his search for her husband and son. He had done his best, but patience was not one of Baron's great virtues, whereas easy money was one of his great vices. The woman had been "filed"; he had made a renewed effort when she had told him of a similar disappearance, and had come up with nothing. Now she had told him that soon the occupant of Brook's Corner would be returning home, and for some reason—perhaps conscience, perhaps slight intrigue—he had decided on one last look, one last scout around the deserted house.

After all, he had nothing to lose; and every piece of information he had so far gathered added up to Absolute Zero.

Baron walked quickly round to the French windows and stood for a moment, surveying the garden area. The door to the woodshed was slightly open, which unnerved him; he hated half-open doors. The garden was half in dawn-shadow, the places beneath the trees, and the high wall that ran beyond them, in darkness. His breath frosted slightly. It was late March, but there was a cold front over England and it felt, at times, like winter.

Baron was suddenly aware that his heart was racing. His life on the streets of East London had taught him many things; and one was that he didn't scare easily; a second lesson was that he always took note of his acute sixth sense, and he felt distinctly that he was not alone.

The garden was still, quiet and deserted. He peered through the windows into the gloom of the lounge, and could see only the shadowy features of furniture, light fittings, and a doorway.

After a moment the frisson of unease had left him; he wiped his hand across his mouth, glancing around once more, then tackled the entry problem.

He was surprised to find that the alarm system was the same as before—which was the system the owner had placed in himself. He would have thought that the caretaker brother-in-law would have had the system changed for a more efficient one. It was the sort of laziness that at once appalled and delighted Baron; it made his job easier, but if he had been a criminal he would have been irritated by the lackadaisical attitude.

As he opened the French windows he again felt the stirrings of unease. It manifested as a prickling on his neck, a breath of air on his face as if a sudden breeze had sprung up. He checked the door to the woodshed, but it was motionless. Zipping his jacket up to the neck, and reaching into his pocket for the secure coldness of a metal cosh, he stepped into the lounge and gently closed the doors behind him.

In the half light, in the cold, he registered a number of things.

The room had been painted brightly; there was still—if he sought for it—the hint of the smell of gloss paint in the air.

A new suite had been brought in; tasteless and uncomfortable looking, the main settee had been positioned on the spot where Brady's comatose body had been found. The last time Baron had been here that particular spot had been marked with tape in the shape of a corpse, just as if the man had been dead.

A vase of flowers stood on the mantelpiece, next to a row of sealed envelopes; welcome home cards, no doubt.

By the door to the hallway, and by the French doors themselves, were two small piles of grey ash, each on a strip of silver-foil paper. Baron stooped and touched the ash with his index finger, smelling it, then touching it cautiously to his tongue. It was bitter, not at all smokey like wood-ash or paper-ash.

But the thing he noticed most of all was the smell, a smell almost powerful enough to block out the odour of paint, though not quite . . . yet potent, nauseating, disgusting nonetheless.

Baron's first impulse was to look for a dead animal, a cat, or rabbit, or something like that, some beast that had been killed in the room a few weeks back and left here. The smell was so putrid that he gagged repeatedly, but he swallowed his gorge and searched behind the furniture, and in the cupboards, but to no avail.

The last time he had experienced such an odour had been some years back when he had discovered the body of a gangland informer. The man had been coated in cement and laid across the joists of an attic, hidden by plasterboard below and layers of insulation above. But the cement had been poorly made, had cracked as the body had expanded, and when the corpse had begun to deliquesce the plasterboard ceiling below had rotted, letting through a thin trickle of almost lethally foetid liquor into the occupied flat below.

Baron's second impulse, then, was to assume the presence of a corpse below the floors. The carpets were not fitted, merely laid on the polished parquet. He was on the point of moving furniture so that he could roll the carpet back and sniff a little harder, when to his astonishment the smell went away.

One second it had been a cloying presence in his nostrils; the next there was only its memory, and the fainter, sweeter smell of paint abounded. Baron straightened and looked around him. The doors were closed, preventing the room from effectively airing; the chimney was open, he supposed. Indeed, the leaf-matter that had been piled into the grate, on top of several green-edged logs, was shifting and stirring as if in a breeze.

Baron shrugged, assumed that his entry into the room had cleared the residuum of some earlier decay, and began a proper patrol.

He worked systematically, rarely bothering with the contents of drawers and cupboards, always looking behind and below them for documents, photographs or any other material that may have been taped to them. He tackled the lounge, then the small study-library. There were too many books here to search inside them all. He opened a few at random, then forced the locked desk-drawers for the second time and skimmed the contents.

He never knew what he was looking for; but like all reasonably successful private investigators he had confidence in his ability to "spot it" when it came up. A torn photograph, not quite fully destroyed for sentimental reasons . . . a phone number, divided up through the pages of a book so that no one, at a glance, would recognize it for what it was . . . a letter tucked away in the sheets of boring looking reports. Very few people were such masters (or mistresses) of deception that they could tolerate having no presence at all in the house of whatever it was they were hoping to keep from their partner. And if the disappearance had in any way been planned, by either Brady or his wife, then there would be *something* around to hint at it.

It was simply a question of finding it.

As he searched, as he worked, he chuckled to himself, remembering what had happened the week before this: investigating a certain business man—on wife's instruction—for infidelity, he had made a routine, covert search of the home, and had thought to look up the open chimney (which was never used). The husband had clearly spent months hollowing out the interior of that chimney to create shelving for what Baron discovered to be the most amazing collection of hardcore pornographic material it had ever been his pleasure to leaf through. The vision that reduced him to helpless mirth was of the balding husband, invisible save for his feet and calves as he stood up the flue of the chimney, trousers round his ankles, just the eerie sound of moaning drifting from the fireplace . . .

There were a limited number of hiding places in any house, but the sheer achievement of that had earned Baron's heartfelt admiration. He gave up on the study, thought briefly of the chimney (which he had checked three months before) but first trotted silently upstairs, and searched the bathroom, bedroom and children's rooms.

He had been in the house for about half an hour, and that was too long. The rooms had been tidied, and quite clearly everything had been searched many times over by the police. Had there been anything to connect anyone in the family with occultism, Black Magic, Satanism, or whatever the chosen term was, it had either been removed, or had never been here.

The only thing that vaguely intrigued Baron had been in the library, and he went back there, now, and stared at the bookshelves.

There were several books on African Mythology, and even more on the occult as practiced by tribes and primitives the world over. Each of these books had Alison Brady's name in them. Inside one, entitled *In the Beginning: Early Man and his Gods*, he had earlier found three thin published papers by Alison Brady herself, all of them from the *Journal of Tropical Agriculture*, and all dealing with the problem of "landscape, industrial development, and supernatural associations with sites." That sentence, in fact, was all he scribbled down in his notebook, the papers' contents being completely beyond him. But he was intrigued by Alison's connection with Africa and "supernatural," even though the papers had been written several years before.

If, as his client would have him believe, the disappearances *were* due to something like witchcraft (and he could scarcely bring himself to think seriously about such a ludicrous idea) then he now had tangible links with the occult from *both* destroyed families: the Brady woman had worked in Africa, or at least had studied African occultism; and the screwy American who had hired him "just to try" (her words) and find her husband and son had, in fact, worked for the Ennean Institute of Paranormal Research.

On impulse, Baron pocketed the three papers, checked the room for anything else African that he might have missed, then returned to the lounge. It was time to go. The day was well advanced, and he didn't want to risk running into the brother-in-law, who might just decide to come in before work and check over the house, ready for Brady's return.

As he was walking to the French doors, he again smelled the foetid odour of corruption. He stopped. The leaves in the fire-grate rustled and stirred. He glanced at them, then around the room.

It occurred to him, then, that for all his thoroughness the one place he hadn't looked for some evidence of a dead bird, or cat, was up the chimney. It would be intriguing to know if something had been slaughtered in some ritual way . . .

He advanced on the fire-grate, stopped, and turned to peer up into the dark shaft. For a second he could see nothing, although a fine dust made him blink. Then, just as his eyes adjusted to the light so that he could begin to distinguish features of brick further up the flue, the wood and leaf litter in the grate exploded into flame.

With an anguished cry Baron staggered back from the roaring fire, striking his head very badly on the brick chimney. He brushed frantically at his clothes and hair, feeling the stinging of burn marks on his neck and chin.

"Christ all fucking mighty!" he yelled, and stared in both bemusement and anger at the leaping flames.

What in God's name could have caused that to light, he thought, and advanced on the fire, watching with a doomed fascination.

The fire leapt higher, licking out of the grate and into the room, driving the investigator back. The flames grew and Baron realized that they were no longer confined to the chimney area. They advanced into the room, swelling and roaring before him, the heat making sweat break out on his face. He felt rigidly held to the spot, unable to turn or run, unable even to cry as he watched, horrified, fascinated . . .

The flame formed into the shape of a giant man, its head broad, leaning down towards him, and in the brilliant yellow of the fire he could sense eyes, a leering mouth, a licking tongue that stabbed at his eyes, half blinding him.

Now he found the energy to turn and run, but the flames were all around him, scorching his clothes and his flesh. He felt his hair ignite and he slapped his hands uselessly at his scalp, screaming all the time. Roasting, burning fire went up inside his jeans, blistering the skin on his legs, burning his genitals, speading upwards inside his clothes until fingers of flame licked out from his leather jacket, joining the conflagration that gathered about the staring, grinning skull of a man more dead than alive, a man unable, now, to do anything to prevent his agonizing consumption by fire.

—SEVEN———————

AT THREE IN the morning, two days after Baron's final investigation, Dan Brady awoke abruptly from a sleep that was tormented by nightmare visions of fire and his family. He had made no sound, of that he was sure, but the anguish he felt at the mind's eye image of Marianna, consumed by flame and crying soundlessly for help, had left him shaken, alert, and saturated with cold, clammy sweat. And for a few moments, as he sat bolt upright in his hospital bed, Brady allowed his body to rack with the sobs that surfaced instantly, exorcising the dream-anguish from his body.

Dim light spilled into his private room from the corridor outside. The hospital was silent, save for a low vibration: machinery gently thrumming out its business deeper in the bowels of the building.

And Brady knew that this was the time to leave.

For a reason more to do with convenience than fear he lay back in his bed as he heard the young Irish nurse walking along the corridor, doing her rounds. The door to his room was opened and Brady feigned sleep. He felt his wrist gently touched, the pulse taken. He breathed easily and deeply, his head turned away from the girl. The moment the door closed behind her he swung his legs out of bed and stood up.

He would have been discharged tomorrow, he knew that. There was nothing keeping him here save doctor's advice. And the police were happy for him to return home too. Sutherland had been in yesterday to interview him again, this time in the presence of a gaunt-looking CID man from Scotland Yard, and a jovial, rather bemused Home Office Official. The interview had taken place in one of the doctor's offices, and in the two hours of close questioning Brady relived the terror and the anguish of the fatal night several times more. He described everything he could remember, sketched the face he had seen, and the hideous amulet. He listed every friend, colleague and relative he could think of, discussed his work, and Alison's work, and her sabbatical in Africa. Eventually, quite exhausted, he had given all he had to give. And now the only thing keeping him here was the medical opinion that after one good night's sleep he would be almost ready to return to active service.

But that dream, and his sudden sedative-free alertness, had left him burningly certain of only one thing:

He had to go home. And he had to go *now*.

He crouched and emptied the locker by his bed. Bill had brought him in some clothes the day before, ready for his official discharge. Jeans, light shoes, heavy check shirt, a short mock-leather windcheater. There was money in one of the pockets: twenty pounds. He hadn't asked for that, but was glad Bill had had the foresight to include it.

He walked to the window as he dressed, opened the blinds, and stared at the lights of the town spread out beyond the hospital.

Out there, he thought. *Among them*.

And the anger that suddenly surfaced made him smash his fist against the window, causing it to buckle and boom with pressure.

Out there, among the lights, among the people, among the innocents . . . out there was his family, three ordinary people malevolently abused and kept from him.

And he would get them back!

He would get them back, he swore so in the Name of the Father, the Good God, and in all the names of Heaven and Hell, and no matter that those names might be on the side of those who had perpetrated the crime . . . he would draw upon all the powers in the known world, and on powers beyond, and he would find Alison, and Marianna, and Dom, and

*return them to their home, and behind them he would leave
lives wasted, and a force of evil crushed . . .*

All this he articulated softly, as he leaned, forehead against
the cold glass, and stared at the lights of the town, and at the
primeval darkness of the countryside beyond.

Out there . . . somewhere out there . . . in the darkness . . .

He realized, almost without thinking it, that he had cried his
last tear, shed the last sorrow in the gentle memory of Marianna. There would be no tears, now, until those he shed with
joy, and relief, when at last—*when* at last—his daughter flung
herself back into his arms, and Alison's embrace hugged them
both, and shy Dominick eagerly grabbed the three of them,
and joined in the celebration.

For the moment, all that Brady could feel was bitterness, a
knot of anger and hate that had swollen to fill every gap in his
body and skull. He had refused sedatives and allowed all emotion to surface and express itself, from violence to hysteria,
from melancholy to panic . . . everything; he had tasted
everything. He had cried for hours, and screamed for hours,
and had thrashed out at anyone who visited, and had sat
silently and mournfully and brooded on the past. He knew,
now, the depth of his commitment to his family, and to their
return. There would never be a moment, not even a second,
during which his life would waver from its dedication to the
return of those three people.

He loved them too much.

And he hated the bastards who had taken them too much to
simply live with his agony, and his grief.

Possessed by love, obsessed with hate. Brady was a child
neither of the Moon nor of Mars, but was torn by these ir-
reconcilable elementals, and out of the pain of that tearing
came an awesome power.

It gave him strength. It gave him direction. It gave him a
concern for three lives which was so potent that it reduced
totally all concern for his own.

It gave him, thus, an invulnerability of mind that would
prove to be his greatest weapon, a sense of immortality that
would eventually free him from ordinary fear.

At ten past midnight he was fully dressed, and finished with

that last moment of sad, bitter reflection. Bill Suchock had
told him to arrive at their house at any time he liked, and
Brady was thinking, vaguely, that he might indeed go to his
sister's. But while the thought of the house at Brook's Corner
was terrifying, because of its memories, it also called to him,
and he acknowledged the need to go there.

He scrawled a quick note on a sheet of paper: *I have discharged myself*.

Smiling thinly at the unintentional implication in those
words, he placed the note on the pillow. It was an inadequate
and discourteous response to a hospital that had nurtured and
cared for him for three months of coma. But it would have to
do. His gratitude could be assumed. But now, without fuss,
without formality, he had to go.

He opened the door into the corridor and stepped quietly
out. Hands in the pockets of his windcheater he strolled easily
towards the stairwell exit, which he knew to be well away from
the nurses' night station, where a uniformed constable was
also seated.

He was just about to push open the double-doors when he
realized there was someone standing on the other side of them.

For a second he was startled. Something like a face had been
peering through the glass from the almost total darkness
beyond, and it had caused his heart to miss a beat, his hand to
hesitate as it reached to the door.

Simultaneously he was aware of the drifting pungency of
some burnt substance, and the edge of his gaze caught a pencil
thin smear on each side of the doors. He touched the marks,
finding them sticky and smelly, and this unpleasant substance
he rubbed on his jeans.

There was no time for further wonder. The moment of surprise, and discomfort, had passed. He pushed through the
doors and into the cold stairwell, ran to the iron bannisters
and peered down six flights into the dim yellow-lit gloom.

The figure that was drifting downwards was tenuous,
smokey, quite insubstantial. It seemed dark grey, with the
feeble yellow light playing on the coils and currents of the fog
that formed the shape. It might have been a man, or some
shambling beast. But it faded rapidly from vision, drifting
downwards, swallowed by the stairwell.

Brady remained frozen to the spot, his eyes wide, his face rigid—not with terror, but with memory . . .

The Smokey Man! Marianna's nightmare, her wild dreams of a figure that had drifted through her room and peered down at her . . .

Perhaps not dreams at all. Unless Brady himself was hallucinating.

The moment of shock passed. Brady fairly flung himself down the stairs, propelling himself off walls and railings, searching the gloom, and the area below, for another glimpse of that bizarre apparition.

He smelled something foetid . . . just briefly, the hint of a smell, like a dead cat in a gutter, or a rat, killed in the woodpile . . .

Then that too was gone.

He reached the heavy door to the car park and stood, breathing hard.

Peering upwards, back towards King George Ward, he could see only darkness, inconsequential emptiness.

Soon he began to doubt the veracity of his own vision. Perhaps, unused to being without sedation, he was inventing images from his own tortured subconscious. Perhaps the Smokey Man had always been a figment of Marianna's imagination, and just briefly had been a figment of his . . .

Why, then, was he so certain, why was his *body* so certain, that what he had seen had been as real as the cold brick wall against which he leaned?

The apparition had been an actuality. It may have been "unreal" in the sense of not being tangible, but it had not been his imagination that had created it. Every ounce of reason that he could summon merely served to substantiate this belief.

There would be no more rationalising away of the inexplicable.

As he gathered his wits about him, and found his breath again, so Dan Brady felt an immediate sense of danger. With a last glance upwards he tugged open the door to the exterior and stepped out into the freezing early Spring night.

Doing up his windcheater as far as he was able, and hunching inside the insubstantial leather for warmth, he trotted quickly across the car park. The moon was at half full, and was clear and bright towards the south. Its brilliance illuminated the bordering trees, and the jagged edges of several small buildings. He made straight away towards the front of the hospital, where bright light spilled from the foyer onto the approach road. There was movement inside the reception area, white coated figures, a nurse or two, citizens waiting out the long night for some change in an emergency admission. Parked close by, he could see a police control car, its two occupants engaged in sleepy conversation, their attention elsewhere.

A single taxi was perched on the rank, its "for hire" sign bright yellow in an otherwise darkened cab. The driver was slumped backwards on his seat, mouth open, breathing loudly. Brady came close enough to hear that noisy slumber, and was on the verge of waking the man up when he realized he didn't want anyone else around him at the moment, not even so anonymous a functionary.

He looked into the darkness. His house was ten miles from the hospital, perhaps eleven.

He could cover the distance in three hours.

And with a last, nervous glance around him, back towards the stairwell exit, he set off to do just that.

He never made it.

After two hours walking through a night which seemed colder than the coldest winter, Brady was exhausted. His legs were aching with fatigue, unused to so much exercise; his body was damp with sweat, and each time he stopped the cold air made his shirt turn to ice—or so it felt. His head began to ache; a knot of tension formed in his breast; his heart raced.

He sat down by the side of the road and tried to *think* some energy back into his limbs. His breath frosted before his face, and the hands that he passed through the fog were white, numb, almost a detached part of his body.

Thought of Brook's Corner made him feel sick. He guessed that part of his distress was because he was not yet ready to return to his home, to the house where the nightmare had occurred.

A car passed by within fifteen minutes, an airline pilot in

less than his usual hurry. He was glad to give Brady a lift, even driving half a mile out of his way so that he could deposit the obviously exhausted man at the steps of his destination.

When Bill Suchock opened the door for the milk at seven that morning his heart nearly stopped with shock as he faced Brady's dishevelled, frozen features, and caught the body as it slumped into his arms.

"Good God man, how long have you been standing there?"

"Not long," breathed Brady, as he limped into the warmth of the centrally-heated house. "An hour perhaps . . ."

"Why didn't you ring?"

Brady smiled feebly. "I did. For about ten minutes. You're heavy sleepers, Bill."

Suchock helped him to the lounge, called for Rosemary, and went to make coffee.

Rosemary fussed around him, trying to make him comfortable, as he ate a breakfast large enough to have fed three, and slowly surfaced from the ice. The boy, Malcolm, stood sullenly by and watched, not communicating with Brady at all after the functional handshake and kiss. Suchock himself rang up his work and said he'd be an hour late. He sat with Brady, quietly, while Malcolm was packed off to school.

When the boy had left, Rosemary seemed to relax, but Brady could see the tension in her face. Normally a clear skinned beauty, with her dark, wavy hair never less than perfectly groomed, Rosemary Suchock now looked harrowed, tired . . . her eyes were rimmed, and there were lines developing at the corners of her mouth; her hair was untidy, even though she had clearly combed it through. As she lit a cigarette, Brady noticed that her hand shook.

She had not been to the hospital to visit him. Clearly this neglect was nagging at her, and she said, "I was going to come and visit today. You jumped the gun on me." Her voice was light, tremulous; she was terribly anxious about having Brady in the house, and Brady glanced at Suchock, who made the merest movement of his head, an unspoken, *don't worry about her, she's okay really*.

"I thought you were up in Durham," Brady said. "Looking after the old boy . . . how is he?"

Rosemary drew deeply on her cigarette, narrowed her eyes

and nodded vigorously, "He's fine, he's really fine. He decided not to come down after all. He sends his love . . . Will you go and see him?"

"Soon," said Brady. "I have things to do . . . I have to go home, first. I have to face that . . ."

Again Rosemary made exaggerated movements of her body, a pronounced affirmation, a desperate attempt to communicate with her brother. She could hardly bear to look at him for more than a second at a time, and she smoked her cigarette as if it was her last. In her housecoat, her pale, thin legs poking through, she looked like a tiny sick child. There was something blocking her, something terrible getting in the way of her relaxation with Brady.

Suchock must have intuited the need for brother and sister to be alone. Rosemary hadn't seen Dan since the tragedy, and clearly her husband's presence was inhibiting Rosemary from expressing that which she most needed to express to her elder kin.

Pure, simple grief.

So Suchock went to make a fresh pot of coffee, closing the door behind him. Brady said to the trembling woman, "How have you been, Rosie?"

She looked down, crushed the cigarette into an ash tray, and began to shake violently, lowering her head even more as the tears squeezed from her. Brady rose and sat beside her, and instantly Rosemary was in his arms, sobbing.

"Oh God, Dan, I'm so sorry . . . so sorry for you . . . for them . . . for your kids. I can't imagine, can't think . . . Oh *Christ*, Dan . . ."

Brady found it hard not to cry himself. He held his sister tightly, stared out the window at the grey, sombre day. "I'm going to find them, Rosie. I'm going to search for them, and I'm going to find them . . ."

Her sobs died away. She looked at him through bleary , red-rimmed eyes, wiped her hand across her face and sniffed. "I'm sorry I didn't come and visit . . ."

Brady repressed the smile he felt. *Same old Rosemary: guilt rules all; self first . . .*

"As I said, I didn't expect it. You'd have come in today . . ."

Her mind, jumping track rapidly as she acknowledged her own selfishness, homed in on what he had said just before. "You're going to look for them? Where?"

Where indeed?

He said, "Wherever impulse takes me. What else can I do, Rosie? I can't live without them; I can't function properly without them. I'm lost without them . . ."

Rosemary climbed to her feet, straightened her housecoat, and began to potter around, gathering up the breakfast things. She had calmed down, wiped her eyes properly, and looked up as Suchock came in with the coffee.

Bill Suchock said, "You know you can stay here as long as you like . . ."

He passed a cup across to Brady, who took it and acknowledged the man with a slight smile. "Thanks, Bill. Thanks both. But I have to go up to Brook's Corner."

Rosemary left the room to get dressed. Suchock watched her go, then glanced at Brady. "She's in a bad way. You'll have to excuse her."

"Nothing to excuse. I know my sister well enough."

"She's haunted. She can't really believe that what has happened *has* happened. And she's been badly spooked by your house. It's a haunted place, Dan. I was there yesterday and I can still feel it. I don't want to upset you or anything, but something is living there . . . take my advice and get a priest in . . ."

"I may well do that." Brady sipped at his cup, thinking vaguely of the house, thinking most about . . .

He shook the images away from his mind. "You've done the lounge up for me, then. That was good of you."

Suchock sat back. "Nothing much. And there's been another fire, a bloody irritating thing . . ." he stared at Brady. "A vagrant, or kids, or something, I don't know what. But there's a patch of burning on the new carpet. You could hide it with a settee or something, but I was bloody furious. Like someone had built a fire in the middle of the lounge. But there wasn't any ash."

"Don't worry about it, Bill. I'm just grateful for all your efforts." He was slightly worried about breaking and entering, though, and added, "Had the doors been forced?"

"Quite expertly. The French windows were open when I arrived. I've closed them, but the lock was broken. I was going to repair it today . . ."

"Never mind," said Brady. "I'll do it myself. It'll help take my mind off things."

Suchock stared at his hands. "It's going to be rough."

"It's rough already."

"I heard you say to Rosie that you're going after them."

"I have no choice. I'll see George Campbell today, or tomorrow . . . sometime, and see if I can't get a few months severance pay. But I can't go back to work. Not yet."

"Are the police . . . I mean, do you think they can be of help?"

"I'm sure they can. I need to know what they know. But I'm not leaving them to search on their own."

Suchock stared at his brother-in-law for a long moment. "If it gets rough, Dan, for Christ's sake don't hesitate . . ."

"As I said, Bill, it's rough already. And I didn't hesitate. And I shan't in future. Thanks."

"I'll come with you to the house."

But Brady shook his head. It was not just that he could divine the reluctance in Suchock's voice, the fervent wish that he didn't *have* to go to the house, it was mostly that Brady wanted to be alone that first time. It had to be faced. He had to know how bad it was going to be . . .

In the event it was not as uncomfortable as he had imagined.

He stood inside the gateway and stared at the blank façade of Brook's Corner. The old lady who lived next door was pottering about in her garden, just visible through the dense stands of trees and bush, where Alison had grown her herbs, and Brady had been building a rockery and proper pond. He didn't draw attention to himself. Instead he strolled along the gravel pathway, round to the right, to where the lounge doors faced the wild garden, its lawn strewn, now, with bits and pieces of furniture, carpeting, rubbish that was left over from the furbishing of the room.

Brady felt a pang of irritation, which he had to temper with gratitude. Bill and Rosemary had worked hard to straighten out the fire damage, he knew; but why couldn't they just have tidied up the traces?

Perhaps it was something to do with their sudden discomfort with the house, the way they felt a haunting presence . . . People who are scared are rarely tidy.

He found the French windows open, as Bill had warned him. Stepping inside, he was instantly aware of the smell of paint. The new furniture was shabby, but functional. The burn in the centre of the carpet was an eyesore.

More immediately noticeable, however, was the tangible sensation of a second presence in the house.

If Brady felt unnerved, even frightened, he suppressed those nerves. Quietly, he closed the doors behind him. He took off his jacket and flung it across the back of an armchair, reached to the grate for a brass poker . . .

He remembered the way the fire had guttered and dimmed . . .

Hefting the poker in his hand he looked around, just to see if there was a more practicable weapon. The paint was a color that he found tasteless. But it was bright at least. He noticed that there was no smoke blur on the ceiling, above the singed carpet. In the fire grate were a few charred logs. Below them, among the ash, he could see a scattering of green pine needles, all that was left of the Xmas tree . . . *crashing to the ground, burning, the tinsel glittering in the flaring light of the fire* . . .

Facing the French windows he stared out into the wind-blown garden. The door to the woodshed was banging open and shut; he noticed that one of the lower branches of the largest of the dead elms had cracked, the limb trailing limply on the ground.

It was cold in the house. He decided to go through and set the central-heating going. And it was as he walked towards the door to the hallway that he heard the sound of someone moving quickly across the main bedroom, above his head.

He froze. His grip on the poker tightened. He wondered, almost idly, if such a heavy weapon would be any use whatsoever against the sort of intangible apparition he had witnessed in the hospital.

What he knew for certain was that it would be most effective against any vagrant, or squatter, who might have taken a liking to the expansive rooms of this deserted house.

But he had been unnerved by the sound, which had died away almost as soon as he had heard it. In the air was the faintest aroma of decay, the unpleasant stink that accompanies a dead animal that has rotted, undiscovered, during a hot summer. The smell, too, passed away, but Brady was left with an uncomfortable sensation of being regarded. He glanced around the lounge, at its shadowy corners, but could see nothing. Movement upstairs caused him to raise his head and stare at the white ceiling. Wind guttered down the chimney, and blew ash into the room, just in front of the grate.

Perhaps it was the wind causing that restless shifting upstairs. Perhaps it was his imagination that supplied the sound of footsteps.

He jerked open the door to the passage, stepped out, walked swiftly to the stairs. Holding the poker at his side he mounted them as quietly as possible. He stepped along the landing to the main bedroom and gently opened the door wide, peering cautiously into the tidy bedroom.

It took moments only to ascertain that the place was deserted; no vagrant, and no ghost, lurked below the bed, or in the wardrobe, or behind the heavy, red curtains.

He walked into the children's rooms, lingering in each, remembering smiling faces, sullen expressions, tantrums, giggling; remembering . . .

The feeling of being watched did not go away. There was a presence surrounding him that was almost tangible. He felt he could speak to it. He felt he could almost touch it. It did not seem, to him, to be hostile. It radiated at him, washing at him from the walls, from the desk in Marianna's room, from the toy box in Dominick's. Wherever he went, walking through the house, he could feel it, and it seemed to embrace him. As he descended the stairs, it followed him, like a cool breeze on his neck, a light ruffling of his hair.

But on the ground floor he felt again that distinct sensation of unease.

He *knew* there was something else in the house with him, something more tangible than ghosts. And whatever it was, he realized as he stood in the hallway, it was in his study.

He could imagine many things, foul and fair, but there was no way that Brady could have known what lay in wait for him as he advanced on the closed door; and so he walked towards it with steady nerve, the brass poker gripped firmly in his right hand. When he reached the door he stopped and listened for a second, then he flung the door open and stepped quickly into the dark room, realizing that the curtains were pulled closed and he could hardly see a thing.

Behind him something moved swiftly toward him, reached out . . .

Brady swung round in terror, his heart almost stopping, his arm raising the poker to strike. Strong hands grabbed his wrist, prevented him from attacking. He found himself staring into a face . . .

A wild face, a face more terrified than his, a face whose every shadow told of despair, and grief, and anger . . .

A woman's face. The face from his coma dreams, the face that had regarded him in sleep.

She was here, in the house. And Brady knew, as he relaxed and let his arm fall to his side, that she had been waiting for him.

─ *EIGHT* ───────────────────

As BRADY CROSSED the study and pulled back the curtains, the woman said, "My name is Ellen Bancroft." Harsh, bright light illuminated the untidy chaos of the room, books pulled from shelves, papers scattered; the drawers of the desk had been pulled completely out and upturned on the floor. Brady surveyed the obvious evidence of this thorough and messy search, and shook his head angrily.

"You do this?"

The woman looked surprised, and stepped away from the door, shaking her head. "No I didn't. But I have a feeling I know who did." Her accent was strongly American; east coast, Brady thought for no particular reason. She seemed slightly angry, staring at Brady as he picked up several books and slotted them back on the shelves. "I'm sorry I broke into your house. But the door *was* open."

Brady glanced at her, then relaxed and smiled. "It seems that my house has functioned like Victoria Station for the last three months. Anybody and everybody has been to have a look."

"This is only the second time I've been here. I was waiting for you."

Strange though that statement should have been, Brady merely nodded. "I know," he said. "When I came home just now I thought there was a tramp camping out in here, or a kid . . ."

"The fire on the carpet," Ellen said, and smiled thinly. "But did you look closely at that burn patch? Is that really how you'd expect a carpet to look after a fire's been built on it?"

Brady walked back towards her, sighing as he glanced around, mentally calculating how much time it would take to straighten this most important of rooms out. This is where he had worked, where Alison had worked. This was the room where they had escaped from the kids and sat and talked privately; in this room, brief though their acquaintance had been with it, they had found a peace of mind together; it was not only their library, it was their parental den, and they would have made such plans together from this dark, cluttered haven . . .

"Yes," he said, "I had noticed. Ellen Bancroft you said?" He extended his hand. Ellen shook hands quickly, almost nervously, as Brady said, "You know my name, I expect . . ."

"Dan Brady. I've known of you for some months."

Brady almost said, "I'm aware of that." The woman looked older than his coma-dream image, and darker skinned; it was either the dusky hue of Jewishness or of many summers tanning in the sort of sun that Alison would have loved, and Brady himself avoided like the plague. She was slimly built, and her hands were quite tiny. Brady found her very attractive. Her dark hair was long and parted simply in the middle. She wore it half covering her face, partly falling across eyes that were deep brown and strangely intense.

He led the way back to the lounge. "Do you know what *happened* to me? To my family?"

It seemed to Brady that the girl shivered. Glancing round, he saw that her complexion had paled noticeably. "I know what happened," she said. "I'm very sorry for you. It's going to take a lot of living with."

"Well I know *that*," said Brady almost irritably. He knew that he was being hostile, when he should have been intrigued. The girl had watched him in hospital, had been waiting for him here, and had been responsible, he was sure, for the continuing strange smells that both he and the hospital staff had noticed . . . she smelled now, very faintly, of a mixture of garlic and burning.

"Sit down," he said, and stooped to dig at the burned logs in the fire. "That's unusual."

"What is?"

"The logs. For a moment I thought they were just covered with ash, but they *are* ash. Burned totally, but still kept their shape . . ." He smashed the dead fire through into the grate, and piled logs high again in the fire place. "Nothing like a wood fire," he said. "Smelly, but exceptionally cosy." He kept his back to her all the while. Ellen just sat and watched him, and he was aware of her scrutiny, and the fact that she was on edge.

When at last he had the fire going he walked to the drinks cabinet, and found that Bill Suchock had stocked it up for him. "What can I offer you? Scotch?"

"Nothing. Thank you. And I suggest that you don't drink anything either. Nothing alcoholic."

Brady was puzzled by that, and stared at the girl's intense expression. "Are you serious?"

"Deadly serious. Alcohol weakens your natural defences. Eat food, eat all the time, and drink coffee if you must; but keep away from spirits. I really mean it . . . Dan."

Perturbed by the girl, and what she was saying, Brady placed the gin bottle down, stared at it, then shrugged and closed the cabinet. "My natural defences," he said, and walking to the fire he prodded the logs with the poker, moving them about so the flames could take more easily. He liked the warm glow that came from the wood; outside, the day was grey and miserable, and a stiff wind blew the empty branches of the trees.

Who the hell *was* this woman? An American; attractive, if slightly dishevelled; smelly; intense. A woman who had been pursuing him since his coma. A woman who talked to him urgently about natural defences, and who was herself bristling with unease, holding her fingers—he noticed as he glanced at her—in strange ways, and whose gaze was a restless, darting thing, her dark eyes never still, always peering over her shoulders, and through the French windows to the cold garden outside.

Brady finally sat down and smiled at Ellen Bancroft. He

didn't quite know what to say to her, so he began obviously.
"New York?"

"I'm from Boston," she said.

"You've come from Boston to find me?"

Ellen laughed. "No. I was working in England up until
October last. I lived here with my husband and son." A
shadow on her face as she said the last words. And instantly
Brady knew! And felt icily cold inside.

He said nothing about it, not wanting to hear the woman
confirm his suspicions. "You visited me in hospital. You even
came into my room. You were dressed as a nurse . . ."

Ellen looked startled. "How could you know that? You
were in a coma. You never even opened your eyes . . ."

"Mysteries, mysteries," said Brady, regarding her keenly.
"But I knew you came, I remembered your face when I woke
up. Whenever you came to the room there was a funny smell,
like burning . . . like the smell in this room now. You suc-
ceeded in puzzling the hospital staff totally. You made them
regard me as something of a sinister freak . . ." he wasn't in
deadly earnest about that, trying a smile as he spoke. But
Ellen's response was severe, almost angry, "At least you are a
live sinister freak. I had to keep you alive, Dan . . . I *have* to
talk to you . . ."

"About what? You have to talk about what?"

"About what happened here . . . in December. About what
you know, what you saw. About how you survived . . . like I
survived . . ."

The wood in the fire crackled loudly, the flames roaring
with a sudden updraught of air. The room seemed to close
around Brady, and he reached out to touch Ellen's hand. She
hesitated just briefly before turning her hand over so that she
could clutch Brady's fingers in hers. They grew close, then,
Brady feeling security from the anguished American, and
Ellen seeming to relax, to be less obsessed with the shadows in
the room.

Letting go of her hand, Brady said, "You lost your family?"

"My husband. My son. In early October."

"Do you want to talk about it?" As he said the words,

Brady felt terror—raw terror. Images from that evil night in December were powerful, saddening, sickening, and he wasn't at all sure if he could cope with hearing an account from someone else of the same attack, of the same horror . . .

But Ellen said, "It's essential I talk about it to you, Dan. And essential you tell me what you remember . . . *everything*. You may not be aware of it, but you are in deadly danger. Even now, even at this moment, I'm aware of it closing in. This house is not defended well enough. Something is already present within it, I can feel it. But it seems to be weakened at the moment . . ." she stopped talking, perhaps aware of the wildly confused look in Brady's face. He was staring at her with all the expression of a child confronted with calculus: baffled bemusement. She had said he was in danger, deadly danger. But danger from what? He asked her as much.

Ellen shook her head. "What do you think? They intended to kill you. They failed. They have left something behind that cannot rest until it finishes the job it began . . ."

Hands on his throat . . . the silence of his attacker, unseen, unheard, just present by its powerful, killing grip upon him . . . and at the last, just a glimpse of it, something more foul than anything he had ever encountered, the product of an evolution that had gone badly, hideously wrong . . . a creature born of darkness, kept alive by fear . . .

Ellen had seen the sudden pallor in Brady's face, and she reached out to touch his hand gently. Brady smiled thinly. "By rights I should have been dead, that much is clear to me."

"And we have to find out how you survived," she said.

"And you? How did you survive?"

Ellen drew her coat around her, as if chilled, despite the warmth from the fire. Her dark eyes flashed bright with memory. Her hands shook as she huddled inside her clothes, and leaned deep into the settee, staring at the burning logs. "I survived because of the weakness of one of them. That much I know almost for sure. And with you, with your strength, I shall be able to confirm that belief. But one of them was weak, and his weakness caused me to be spared . . . at least in one way . . ."

. . . the day before had been bright, sunny, and wonderfully hot. Ellen had walked the mile to work in her lightest clothes: it was shirt-sleeves weather, and for late September, and in England, she thought that was pretty good.

And as if to catch her out in her gluttony of satisfaction, autumn had dawned the next day with the greyest, dullest sky imaginable; the heavens had opened, and the countryside around the Ennean Institute of Paranormal Research had been bathed in a monotonous, drenching rain. It had rained from early morning until the early evening. Ellen had fled home on public transport and had arrived at her apartment soaked to the skin, dishevelled, and very, very cold.

Her son, Justin, was home from school, sulking in his room, and pretending to do his homework. The rain beat against the windows, poured through guttering, and seemed to fall from a sky that grew darker, more ominous, by the minute. On evenings like this she felt like doing nothing; it was not that she felt cold, nor that she disliked rain in itself, but this English autumn weather was so morbid, so miserable, it drained the spark of fun from her, sapped the spirit level, reduced her—and her son, and husband Michael—to morose, unsociable spectres.

She changed her clothes, and sat down at her dressing table to comb through her damp hair. "Make coffee," she shouted to Justin, and heard his grumpy reply, indicating his feelings to the negative.

"Coffee!" she yelled, and waited, listening for his feet, stomping heavily down the corridor to the kitchen. "Strong!"

It was as she became finally satisfied with her hair again, and sat staring in the mirror at her reflection, vaguely distressed with the effect England was having on her tan, on her skin and on her every physical feature, that the hair on her neck prickled, and she swung round on her stool, staring wide-eyed round the bedroom.

The rain clattered against the window like pebbles thrown from the gardens outside. The bedroom was warm, lit only by the light from her dressing table, and was otherwise shadowy and grey. For a second she had *distinctly* felt that someone had entered the room.

With the blood pounding in her temples she waited. Part of her was definitely responding to something inside the room.

She couldn't see it, hear it or smell it, but somehow she was registering its presence, and it was scaring the life out of her.

She rose to her feet, self-consciously tugging down her white slip, and walked towards the window. The touch on her leg, when it came, freaked her totally. She screamed, twisted, and backed away, fetching up hard against the wall.

She brushed at her thigh and tried to calm down, but she was panic-stricken, and terrified. The touch had been that of a hand, a large, heavy hand, its fingers digging briefly into the flesh of her leg. She could still feel the pressure of the thumb, the sharp edges of nails. A tickling sensation—the briefest memory—told her of hairs on the wrist.

If Justin had heard her scream, he had decided to ignore it. It was not the first time in recent weeks that he would have heard sounds of distress from his mother's room, and having been told that "everything was all right" twice before, he had no doubt decided to let the woman get on with things.

But Ellen was so shaken she would have loved for Justin to come running in at that moment, and fling his arms around her.

She stood by the window, listening to the rain, to the sound of cups clattering in the kitchen. There was a sudden, tentative pressure on her stomach and she closed her eyes, bit her lip, and tried to stifle the cry of anguish that she felt surfacing. After a second she began to slap at her stomach, trying to drown that ghostly pressure with the pain of her own violence. The pressure increased, the sensation of a hand on the sensitive skin of her belly, its fingers spreading so that one of them touched her navel, making her wince and cry with despair; another finger touched the base of her stomach, moved through her pubic hair; the hand slid downwards, touching her intimately, tentatively, making her body recoil and twist as sensations of arousal mixed with the shocked reverberation of horror. Her muscles spasmed; her skin crawled; it was terrifying, invisible assault.

At last the pressure went away. She ran from the bedroom, into the bathroom, leaned across the sink and was violently sick. She stripped naked and washed herself repeatedly, all the time terrified that those spectral fingers would touch her again. Justin heard the sound of her vomiting and timorously called through the bathroom door, "Are you all right?"

"Just make that coffee," she called back.

She washed her face, dried her body, dressed in slacks and a heavy jumper. Her hands shook violently as she sipped her coffee, staring at her silent son, but after half an hour or so she felt calm enough to smile, relaxed enough to start preparing a light supper.

Michael arrived home an hour later. He was tired; that was to be expected, this having been an important day for him at his firm. He kissed Ellen, dumped his bag and his coat, then flopped down in an armchair.

"Spaghetti and meatballs," Ellen announced from the lounge doorway. She leaned against the jamb and stared at her exhausted husband, wondering whether or not to tell him of what had happened. She had told him on each of the previous occasions and he had seemed sceptical, if slightly concerned for Ellen's mental well-being.

But what else could he have said to a woman who complained of ghostly "touching"? The apartment was in a new block, quite unlikely to be haunted. And although he had been experiencing nightmares, and restless sleep for the past two weeks, he had attributed that to tension over his work for the oil company. He was under a lot of pressure, and was almost reluctant to admit to the headaches, the pressure in his chest, the periods of disorientation.

He would have to admit it tonight. He looked quite ill, quite frighteningly pale.

"I'm not hungry," he said. "Sorry. I should have rung."

"What's the matter, Michael?"

He shrugged, glanced up to her and smiled, and that smile was a wan, uncertain thing. Ellen immediately came over to him, knelt by the chair and kissed him. "Tension," he said. "I feel very shaky. Flu maybe; a virus."

"Is it the same as before?" She felt a coldness on her skin, a deep chill; it was shock, like the shock of being told a favourite friend is dead. She was calm, thinking clearly, yet every muscle in her body was reacting to what she could see, what she could hear.

Michael Bancroft was a broad-shouldered, strongly-built
man, dark of complexion, handsome, strong-eyed. He was
like a child, now, a huddled, despondent child. He banged at
his chest with his fist, as if the ache, the tension, would go
away.

"A little worse, perhaps. God, Ellen . . ." he struggled to
frame the words in his mouth, his eyes filling with tears.
"God, tell me I'm too young to have a heart attack. I'm
thirty-eight years old. Surely . . . surely that's too young?"

"Much too young," she said reassuringly, and leaned forward to kiss his cheek. "It's tension, Michael. It's something—even if it's not tension—that you can *do* something
about . . ."

*We've got to get out of here. We've got to leave, before it's
too late. They're closing in. How do I convince him that we
must leave? Oh Christ, it's getting closer, I know it, I know
it . . .*

Michael must have seen the look of anguish on Ellen's face.
He wiped a broad, muscular hand across his eyes, sniffed and
smiled. Then he reached out and hugged her, kissing her cold
ear. "What is it? You look upset."

Ellen drew back, touched Michael's face with her hands;
looking at him, seeing the concern in his face, the quick way
which he dismissed his own problems and focussed on what he
intuited was a difficulty with her, she couldn't help feeling a
warm rush of affection; she loved him so much. Their marriage was rough, rocky, the inevitable consequence of people
from two different cultures marrying and settling in the homeland of one of them. But God, how she loved Michael, how
she fed from his strength.

"Michael . . . I don't know how to say this, how to convince
you, but . . . we must leave. We *must* leave. We're in danger, I
know we're in danger. I can feel it. What's happening to you,
and the awful things that have been happening to me . . ."

"The touching," he said. "Has it happened again?"

"When I came in this evening. It was more powerful than
before, more lingering. I was sick afterwards, really sick. I'm
not imagining it, Michael. It's happening to me, a real attack.
Just like . . . just like the attack on you."

There! It was said. He would have to know, and now the moment was done, the first words spoken.

Michael stared at his wife quizzically. "What does that mean? Attack? You don't mean an attack of 'flu . . . or heart . . . what the hell are you talking about?"

He knew. He was just unprepared to say it.

"Psychic attack. You know what I mean, I can tell."

"Oh come on, Ellen. Psychic attack . . . by whom? Someone at the Ennean? Someone jealous of me? Or jealous of you? What the hell are you people working on down there, anyway?"

Ellen placed a hand gently on his mouth. She shook her head, but tried to keep her expression one of understanding and friendliness, even though she felt like screaming at the man, screaming at him to find some common sense. "Don't make light of it, Michael. And don't dismiss it. Everything that's happening to you, every symptom . . . the pain, the tension, the dizziness, the loss of appetite, it's all part of the pattern. Somewhere, someone is attacking you. If they stay at a distance, then we can fight back. But they're attacking me too, although in a way that makes no sense. They're wearing us down, weakening us. What for, Michael? Why are they doing it? We've *got* to get away. Let's pack right now and go, leave the country. Let's go abroad. Let's distance ourselves . . ."

"Just like that!" Michael snapped his fingers, grinned and shook his head. "You know I can't leave work just now. Promotion looms before me, and with it, luxuries unheard of. Psychic attack . . ." he laughed, ruffled Ellen's hair as she knelt beside him, looking exasperated. "I'm tired, tense, exhausted . . . I'm apprehensive. That's all it is."

"I'm going to lose you . . ." said Ellen weakly, and she felt instantly depressed, instantly drained. Michael's rejection of her urgent plea had left her weakened, but now, almost as if the thought was as inevitable as rain in September, she sensed deep within her that she and her husband were lost to each other.

She rose to her feet, walking mechanically, almost numbly, out to the kitchen. Michael came behind her, and though he seemed more jovial now, Ellen could see that he was still touching his chest, still labouring for breath; the dark lines about his eyes could not be banished by his simple, cheerful demeanour.

"I'm hungry now," he said. "I've got my appetite back. I'll just go and freshen up."

They sat silently at the table and ate spaghetti, with meatballs that burned the back of the throat, since Ellen, without thinking, had made them with chilli powder. Justin ate only three, then pushed his plate away. Ellen listened to the driving rain, feeling chilled to the marrow.

"Why don't we go out for a drink?" said Michael, leaning back in his chair. He waved his hand in front of his mouth. "A cooling pint of lager." He smiled as he spoke.

Ellen was quite agreeable to the suggestion, although the thought of venturing out in that rainstorm wasn't the most inviting idea. But anything to get out of the apartment for an hour or so.

She rose and gathered up the plates. A car drove along the roadway outside the block of flats, and its headlights struck the dining room window, eerily silhouetting the small trees that bordered the gardens. And Ellen dropped the plates in shock.

There was a man standing outside.

The light passed away, and there was just darkness beyond the rain-soaked window. Ellen crossed the room quickly and closed the curtains, reaching between them to lock the double-glazing . . .

In the bedroom, the window was flung open. A vase, which she knew had been standing upon the bedside table, crashed to the floor with the wind that swept into the room. She could hear the rain driving in, the curtains flapping.

"What the hell?" Michael got to his feet, walked down the corridor towards the bedroom . . .

"Michael!" screamed Ellen, and he stopped, and turned. Justin had risen to his feet and was staring at his father, then at the dining room window, and his face was a mask of shock, all muscles tense, all blood draining.

The lights went out.

The dining room window exploded inwards, rain, wind and something ice-cold and painful sweeping into the suddenly darkened room. Michael came running back along the corridor, screaming Ellen's name. She felt herself picked up and flung bodily against the wall. Justin's screams turned suddenly into strangled whimpers, and then he was silent.

Light flickered in the room, a torch she thought. In the instants before it was knocked from Michael's hand she glimpsed, by its thin, yellow beam, the horrors that had swarmed into the flat, creatures that walked upright, yet peered at her with the glittering eyes of animals, faces leering in bovine or reptilian ways, mouths wet and grinding. They were visions of demons, grotesque distortions of nature, and their horny, scaly hands plucked at her flesh, and struck down repeatedly at Michael and Justin.

She heard words, names, laughter. A wind literally howled through the room, freezing the blood in her veins. She glimpsed Justin's body as it was held up and flung across one of the creatures' shoulders. She could hear Michael struggling, and the steady, sickening sound of flesh yielding to animal blows.

Rough hands picked her up, but when she struck out in front of her she could feel nothing. She heard laughter. Justin moaned and she screamed his name, and he cried out . . . "Mummy!" and it was the last sound she heard him make before he was carried through the window.

The hands moved from her throat to her breasts, and she squirmed away and ran across the room. She hit a dark figure, and inhaled the moist stench of its breath as it laughed and flung her away.

"Kill her quickly. Quickly!" came the words.

"Disturbance upstairs," said a woman's voice.

"Quickly! Quickly!" came the repeated command, and she felt hands groping for her.

Screaming with all her might, Ellen scratched down, and struck at the cowled beast that was trying to wrestle with her. Glistening saliva drenched her hand. She flung off its grip and leapt towards the window, tripping on the sill so that she fell heavily on the rain-sodden turf of the garden outside. Immune to pain, her head filled with the sound of her family's cries, she struggled to her feet and began to run.

Behind her she heard a whoop of amusement, a cry, a command. And she heard the heavy sound of a footfall as of someone in pursuit.

Screaming for a car, desperate to see something or someone who could help her, she ran through the stinging rain, scarcely able to see as the storm blew icily against her. Her legs pumped and she ignored the terrible ache in her muscles. She ran as fast as she was able, but the wind slowed her down, and her drenched hair insisted on flopping into her eyes, blinding her.

When she stopped for breath, in the full glow of a street-lamp, she heard the sound of pursuit, glanced round and saw no man, nor even an animal. But she could sense the giant shape that followed her by the way the rain beat around it, running along its outlines: whatever it was it was monstrous, grinning, and closing the distance on her with amazing speed.

She ran again, tripped, struggled and kept moving. Her voice could hardly find the strength to cry, now, and she abandoned the idea of calling for help. She prayed for a police car, or a lorry, or *anything* that could take her away from the horror that loped after her.

Everyone was indoors, huddled in the safety of their homes, away from the miserable, wet night.

At last she could run no more. She stopped, breathed deeply, wiped hair from her eyes, and screamed with every ounce of strength left in her body.

She was still screaming when hands grasped her by the legs and swung her bodily from the ground, flinging her down onto the grass kerb. As she tried to struggle to her feet she felt an immense weight lay upon her, smelled a stink that made her gag, waited for the hands to clench around her throat. To a passer-by she would seem to have been lying there alone, legs apart, struggling, hands beating at thin air. She felt herself touched, handled, probed. She saw her blouse ripped away, her jeans torn, stripped down each leg in turn. Her flesh bled, bruising before her eyes as the hands slapped and beat at her; but all the time that invisible touch returned to her breasts, and to her groin.

And then, as abruptly as it had arrived upon her so that abhorrent presence went away. She was hardly aware that it had gone, her body continuing to rack and shake with cold and pain. She thought she would feel those fingers forever. Slowly it occurred to her that the only touch upon her naked body was the bitter touch of driving rain. She sat up, wiped her hair from her face, looked down at herself; by the yellow glare of the neon lamp she watched the blood from her scratches mingling with the pure water.

She reached for her tattered blouse and pulled it around her shoulders. Her jeans had been neatly torn in two, but she pulled them on like leggings, holding them at her waist.

Thus, ungainly yet alive, she staggered back through the rain, back through the night, to face the ruin of her apartment flat.

And the emptiness.

— NINE

THE RECOUNTING OF the horror to Brady had finally reduced Ellen to tears, and if Brady were honest with himself, it was only his attempts to console the woman that stopped him crying himself.

She had spoken slowly, and at times with a confusion and an incoherence that Brady could both understand and sympathize with. It had left him a little dizzy, slightly unsure of some of the sequences and events. More importantly, it had made him shiver with the familiarity of it; what had happened to Ellen Bancroft had been precisely what had happened to him and his family, from the earlier sense of being watched, monitored, or whatever he chose to call it, to the cold words, "Kill her. Quickly."

Those who were not needed could not be left to their own devices, to their sadness. They had to be killed.

And in two cases—and the policeman, Sutherland, had hinted at there being only three incidents that he knew of—in two cases that killing had failed. Ellen had already referred to a weakness in one of the group, and that word, weakness, was a peg on which Brady began to pin a great hope.

"Under the circumstances," he said, as Ellen finally stopped her silent weeping, and dabbed at her face with a tissue, "I think a drink is called for. Just one can't do any harm, can it?"

Ellen glanced at him angrily, her eyes red, and sparkling

with moisture. "For Christ's sake, Dan. Don't turn out like Michael. He wouldn't listen to me. He wouldn't do what I said he should do. I beg you. Until you know better, believe that what I say is true . . . don't drink alcohol, in any form, in however small a quantity."

Brady was impressed by the woman's earnest plea, and the confidence of her words. He nodded quickly, accepting her ruling. "Coffee, then. Strong coffee."

"I think I need it. Black. No sugar."

A few minutes later, when she sipped her drink and stared at the crackling fire, she sketched in the events of the few weeks after the attack on her.

"I couldn't stay in the flat. A friend of mine took care of the selling of it and also helped me find an apartment in London, somewhere out of the way. It was a grotty place, as Michael would have said. Small, dirty, in bad need of decoration, but it was just what I needed. I moved everything I needed into it, and established defences around it . . ."

Brady frowned. "What sort of defences?"

Ellen made a sniffing motion as she stared at Brady.

Brady grasped her meaning. "Little piles of ash; smears; funny smelling substances . . .?"

"All part of it, Dan. Psychic defences. How else do you defend against psychic attack? You can't lock doors, or put up barbed wire, or sleep with a double-barrelled shotgun next to you. I turned that little flat into a fortress. Inside it, for a while, I'm safe. Outside, I can be targeted. I'm being targeted now, I'm sure, but it's not close. You are targeted too, Dan, and you're in deadly danger . . ." She gulped coffee. Brady stared at her, then glanced uneasily outside, into the garden; the afternoon was well advanced. It was a cloudy day, and the gloom was descending. "Do you think we should get out of here?"

Ellen shook her head. "We're in danger, but it's not imminent. Trust me, Dan. There's something here . . ." she frowned as she looked around the room. "But I don't understand what. It's not as strong as I remember it. When I first broke into the house, with someone's help, I could sense a powerful force of destruction. It threatened me badly, and frightened me. But it's not so strong now."

"You're losing me, Ellen . . ."

She smiled, appreciative of Brady's struggle to learn, and of the way she was jumping from subject to subject. She picked up where she had left off. "My flat is a haven. We must transform this whole house into a haven, Dan. It's big, it has a huge garden. Ideally it should be a town house—elemental forces work more potently in the country. But I don't think it matters. The house is defendable. But one immediate defence is this: *don't trust anyone*. Don't depend on anyone at all. Not even family. When I quit my work I didn't go back, I didn't show my face at the building again. I had one friend, one man who I *had* to trust. Perhaps we all need just one close friend, one person whom we must hold above suspicion. I needed him, and he helped me in so many ways that I can probably never repay the debt. And he hasn't breached that trust, and I think you can trust him too."

"When do I meet him?"

Ellen smiled. "You've met. He's at Hillingvale. Andrew Haddingham."

"My PSO!" said Brady, surprised totally, then explained, "Principal Scientific Officer".

"I'm familiar with Civil Service ranking," Ellen said. "As I told you, I ran a team at the Ennean Institute. I worked with Geoffrey Dean, the famous *Professor* Geoffrey Dean. When I say worked with him I should say *I* worked, and every month when he surfaced from his Devonshire estates he would read my notes, grunt, and later use my results for some talk or other. To watch us you would think he hardly knew I existed."

"And your work?"

"Mainly psychic manifestation, especially apportations. That's—"

"Carrying objects through space and time. I know."

"I was also part of the liaison group set up between the Ennean and Hillingvale, comparing notes, swapping ideas. I knew most of the department chiefs at the Station. I even remember seeing you, on occasion. But I was closest to Andrew Haddingham."

Brady was catching up fast. "In fact, I think he may have talked about you. And it was Andrew who told you about the incident . . . here. The attack on me."

"He told me immediately. He was very distressed, Dan. I think he regards you as a good friend, and you can trust him. I'm sure you can. He told me where you'd been taken, and I realized that you wouldn't survive a second attack. It was still incomprehensible to me that you could have survived the first."

"So you came to the hospital, scattering your ashes, and smearing your herbs. You set up defences around my room . . . Good God." Brady was impressed. He watched Ellen closely.

"I set them up around the whole ward," she said. "Defences have to be set up in zones. I protected your bed, your room, and the whole area. There were three killings on the ward . . ."

"So I heard."

"The Stalker—you probably heard that word, or thought-form, or *fetch*, something like that—the Stalker broke through the outer defences on two occasions, and expended its violence on other patients and two nurses, I think. It couldn't get close to you. It's one of the most terrifying things about this particular attack . . . the thought-form does not retire if it fails, it strikes out around it. The projection is immensely powerful, but similarly, it weakens quickly."

Brady understood. "Because the man who is creating it grows tired."

"*Very* tired," agreed Ellen. "He's doing too much . . ."

"Or *she* is . . . It could be a woman behind it."

But Ellen shook her head, quite emphatically, "It's not a woman. It's a man. I can't be totally sure, I just . . . well, I'm ninety-nine percent sure. It weakens so quickly because, firstly, just creating a thought-form is draining on the body's energy. Second, this man is targeting the Stalker on two people. The thought-form that has been stalking *me* is the same one that is now targeting on you. When I came to the hospital, maybe the third or fourth time, the thing was there. I sensed it; I even saw it, interacting with the light in the stair-well. I recognized it at once."

Brady rose from his armchair and placed a new log on the dwindling fire. It was not that it was particularly cold in the room, just that the flickering wood fire was a warm cosy focus for his attention during this bizarre indoctrination. "So our man, the man trying to kill us, is dividing his effort, and this is crippling him slowly."

"That's right."

He said, "Can you *see* the man? Can we go to him? Can we find him?"

He was thinking: *He's one of them. He's one of those who were here that night. The first. He was here as mind alone, but he was here, and he will be the first. I must find him.*

"Not yet," said Ellen. "The image isn't strong enough . . ."

"But you're aware of him to a degree, then?"

Ellen shivered. Brady glanced round, aware of that moment of intense discomfort. She said, "I'm beginning to suspect. It's what I meant by the weakness. The man is dividing his projection, and that must be making him quite exhausted. He's also reluctant to kill *me*. Three or four times the Stalker has done no more than sexually assault me. Psychic assault, and so far it has held back from a full attack."

"The man wants . . . what? To rape you? He has that sort of violence in mind?"

"It's more subtle than that. He knows me and he is experiencing desire for me, strong feelings of love. When the thought-form attacks it responds to the unconscious wishes of the man creating it, and instead of killing . . . it feels, it tries to make love. Each encounter has grown in determination." She was pale-faced and huddled, sitting on the edge of her chair, the empty cup cradled in her hands. Brady remained crouched by the fire, watching her.

"And if it strikes again?"

"It will complete the deed," she said. "And I dread that. I feel sick even thinking about it." Her eyes, fixed on the fire, were narrowed, and Brady could intuit something of the pain she was feeling. "I dread it," she repeated in a whisper. "It's the most vile thing . . . I think it would be better to be killed."

"But you are protected, now. You know how to protect yourself."

"To a degree, yes. I've researched the subject very hard. But there is something wrong, something *weird* in this attack. There's an uncontrolled feel about it, which worries me. Is that a strength or a weakness? I just don't know."

Ellen stood, quite abruptly, and placed the cup on the mantelpiece, crossing the room to stand by the French windows.
Her arms were folded across her chest, and Brady could see
that she was shaking. She was smaller than Alison, but seen in
half silhouette against the fading day there was something
familiar about the way her hair fell about her shoulders; that
hunched stance, cold, almost angry, was the way Alison had
often stood when they had rowed, or when she had been
deeply upset, denying Brady's efforts to pacify her.

His head was literally throbbing, that uncomfortable sensation of heart-blood surging through the skull, when the blood
pressure is high, and the mind is clear, cold, aware. In his
stomach he felt a churning knot of sickness and tension. He
realized that he was forcing the memory of Alison's bestial
treatment from his mind. But it was impossible not to remember, and though he kept the tears back, for a long minute or
two he leaned against the mantelpiece, above the fire, and
shook and shook, his attention half on the floor, half on the
silent woman by the windows.

From the garden, Ellen Bancroft was a dimly seen shape, her
features highlighted from behind by the flickering fire. From
the woodshed, no details of her face were visible. Beyond the
woodshed, where the trees cast shadows on the lawn, any
watcher might have had difficulty in telling whether it was a
man or a woman who stood there, staring morosely out into
the late afternoon.

By the high wall, sixty yards from the house, there was a
place where dead wood and decaying leaves, piled there before
Christmas, still formed a substantial mound. From here,
Ellen's figure was a dimly perceived shape, which abruptly
turned from the window and retired into the room. She most
certainly could not have seen the wall from where she had been
standing, and she would not have noticed the slumped,
charred figure that was half buried in this compost.

Nor would she have noticed its hand rise from the leaves,
wood tumbling as it sat upright, burned eyes staring blindly at
the house.

•   •   •

They went upstairs, and stood by the window in Marianna's room, peering out across the garden towards the neighbouring residence where old Mrs. Dalby lived.

Ellen was still cold, her hands shaking. "There *is* something here," she said, turning back into the room and leaning against the sill. She stared at the dolls piled up on the small cupboard, and at the childish pictures on the wall. Pushed into a corner were the papier-mâché models which Marianna had produced during the autumn. The room was tidy but lived in. To Brady, holding back his emotions as best he could, it seemed inconceivable that the untidy little girl would not come squealing and giggling into the room, and leap onto her bed, bouncing up and down as she greeted her father.

Brady shook the memories away. "I feel nothing," he said. "It worries me. Perhaps I should try and develop some psychic talent."

"You almost certainly have a degree of talent," said Ellen.

"And do you?"

"Yes. A little. I have what Hillingvale calls PPS-Passive Psychic Resonance. We call it Echo Respondance." She stared around the room, then reached out to pat the outside wall. "The wall is cold. This isn't all brick, is it? It's stone, a lot of stone. Stone absorbs. Stone traps. Stone records."

"And you can become aware of that absorption?"

Ellen nodded, as she tapped the wall with her knuckle. "It's confused and shallow, but I sense it. In the garden too. There's a focus of psychic entry below your garden—a well, perhaps, or part of an older house. I can't tell where exactly."

Brady thought hard for a moment, intrigued by what Ellen was saying. "How about a Roman settlement? Could that be it?"

"Here? Most certainly. Why do you say that?"

Brady pointed to the distant pinewoods. "Below that woodland. There's thought to be a villa. A bit of it was found in the eighteenth century and lost again, but it's never been excavated."

Ellen smiled. "Well there you are. I think part of it at least is underneath your grounds. That'll help—"

"Help? In what way?"

"You'll see."

Brady thrust his hands into his pockets and stared at the plastered wall of the room. "So you're saying that the 'presence' that scared Bill, and you, might be part of the thought-form that attacked me and which is still trapped in the stone?"

But Ellen didn't know for sure. "What I felt when I came here before was almost tangible, some *living* thing, moving freely through the house. It watched me, but it didn't attack me. It didn't go away when I set up some simple defences. If it isn't an echo of the elemental that attacked then I can't think what it could be, but it didn't seem powerful enough to do any harm. It scared your brother-in-law. It terrified the man I employed to work for me."

"Who was that?"

"A private detective, a very unsavoury man, as the English would say. And unreliable. I never met him, but I observed him. Andrew set the thing up. The man's name was Baron, but he was useless. He discovered nothing that I hadn't discovered myself when he tried to find Michael and Justin. And here, well . . . nothing either."

"Just a ghost," said Brady quietly. "The Stalker, waiting for my return. But it didn't wait long enough."

"It may have decayed. That invariably happens to unbound psychic substance. It fades away . . ."

As they walked back down to the kitchen, Brady's thoughts were in a turmoil. There was so much he didn't understand, and so many things that he wanted answers to, and one question which nagged was the coincidence he now faced. Could it *really* be simple coincidence that the two survivors of attacks on three families happened to both work in the field of the paranormal? Had he and Ellen in some way drawn attention to their families *because* of their work, set their families up as easy targets for the men who had taken them?

But the thought which was foremost in his mind was that the man behind the Stalker was both a danger to be suppressed, and a source of information that he needed. He was a hunter now. There was nothing left for him but the search for Alison and his family, and that search could not begin until the Stalker was destroyed. The man who had projected the thought-form was one of them, but there were so many others, and he had so little to go on. He could vividly see the amulet with its screaming head, the warped labyrinthine pattern, the hideous face of the mongol, the jewelled phallus used by the black-robed woman. The details in his mind were crystal clear, but without some hint as to where to go first, they were just so many memories.

He *needed* the man behind the Stalker. He would kill him—what else could he do? The thought of it filled him with nothing more than a vague unease, for it would be no worse than killing a vicious animal. But before he dispatched that first of the enemy, the man had to be made to talk. He *had* to talk.

And Brady knew that to get to that source and extract information from him, he had to understand the nature of psychic attack far better than he did.

"This thought-form . . . . it hits but it cannot be hit."

"That's right."

"It strangles, but it cannot be strangled. It can be felt on the body, but when you feel for it . . . there's nothing."

"That's right."

"It can be seen under certain conditions."

"Ordinary people can't see it. If you're the target you can see it sometimes, especially if you're tired. And if you have some slight psychic awareness, the inner vision that some people have, you can glimpse it too. Other targeted people see thought-form as shadowy presences."

"But non-targeted people can still be killed, be touched. They can be made aware of the Stalker, and affected by it."

"That is what is so strange about this case. Such non-targeted aggression is something I've never heard of, nor read of before. Its consequences are very frightening."

When Brady said nothing, waiting to hear what exactly she meant, Ellen said, "It sounds as if the power generating this Stalker is using an unfamiliar technique, perhaps a new technique, perhaps a more ancient one. Whatever is happening, the Stalker seems to behave independently of its master. My fear is that it will become detached from him; that it will function totally independently, that it will no longer be affected by its master's own power, fading when he grows tired, only pursuing us when he is actively concentrating on the task of pursuit."

"How well will your defences function then?"

Ellen shrugged. "I wish I knew. All psychic attack works from mind to mind; all defence against such attack is designed ultimately to affect the *mind* behind the attack. I just wouldn't know what to do if the thought-form became *detached* from its creator. Which is why the sooner we set up proper defences around the house the better. We shall have to do a lot of learning from experience . . ."

But Brady was more positive. "We have to get to the man behind the attack, before his minds gets to us. But how do we get an idea of who it is? How do we see him?"

Ellem smiled almost cynically. She crossed her arms and stared beyond Brady, perhaps seeing nothing at all but her own anxiety. "There is a way," she said. "I've already mentioned it. It's just that . . ." her gaze, turning suddenly on Brady, was intense and terrified, almost pleading. "I can't face it. I couldn't face it . . ."

Brady knew what she meant, and there was no doubt in his mind that the solution—that she should actually encourage another attack by the Stalker in an attempt to psyche out the man behind the projection—was a solution that could not be entertained.

At least, not by him on Ellen's behalf.

Changing the subject quickly, before Ellen's anxiety turned to melancholy, Brady said, "So is this Stalker the way psychic attack always works?"

"Commonly," she said, "but not exclusively. In its commonest form, psychic attack is simply the willing, from some distance, of debilitating and distracting effects upon the victim: headaches, dizziness, lack of concentration, depression, hallucination and physiological changes that result in death."

"Sounds familiar," said Brady lightly. "Also sounds like a hangover."

Ellen smiled. "Worse than a hangover. Anyway, this simple psychic attack can be given *shape*, human or animal form. They become artificial elementals. There's a form called the Watcher—what it sees, hears and smells becomes known to the man creating it as soon as the psychic substance is resorbed. Then there's the Stalker, which is strong and destructive. You need special defences against a Stalker, but imagination is one of the best."

"How?"

"Things *created* by the mind, can be destroyed by the mind," she said.

"If the mind is strong enough."

"Exactly. The strongest thought-form is generated by several minds. It's persistent and independent, but weak in other ways. All this generation requires great concentration by the assailant, including a period of fasting and meditation on the hatred felt for the victim. And at some time, parts of your bodily exudates will have been obtained. Your hair, nails, almost certainly your blood and urine. And semen."

Brady was astonished. "How on earth would they have got a sample of that?"

Ellen shrugged. "Many ways. Your wife's clothing; tissues not adequately disposed of; your sheets; a medical. Haven't you had a medical recently?"

"May of last year. I *did* give a sample for a sperm count. That's a horrifying thought . . ."

Ellen went on, "You'll have had a sample of your clothing stolen, and a mannikin made from the material, with all the exudates incorporated."

"Witchcraft," Brady said. "It sounds like witchcraft . . ."

Ellen just smiled at that. "If you like. But it's sympathetic magic. A focus for the attacking mind; a scent for the powerful force that the mind creates."

"Then the attack begins . . ."

She nodded. "First the ordinary symptoms, dizziness and all that. Then a Watcher to explore the victim's location. Then the Stalker to kill. The horror of the Stalker is that it exists both as a projection from the *attacker's* mind, and as a nightmare belief in the victim's. When the two things come together the victim helps create the Stalker in its true horror, seeing a foul face, a terrifying shape, reacting to it with *acceptance* and not the scepticism that would weaken it. Soon after, it strikes, often disembowelling or decapitating, or crushing the victim to a pulp."

"It still sounds like witchcraft," said Brady, staring out at the darkening garden. A neighbouring cat had leapt onto the window-sill and stared in for a moment, and Brady had been distractedly thinking of his own two cats. What had happened to them? "But I know it's not. My darling little gerbils were sending short bursts of extrasensory energy to each other in times of great danger. I'm not surprised that the human mind needs something to focus onto for its concentration."

Ellen was looking tired. She leaned against the sink, biting her lower lip thoughtfully. After a moment she asked, "And did you have any of those symptoms? Any unusually persistent headaches?"

"Yes I did. Migraines, very bad. Since about July. And indigestion. And I didn't sleep well through the autumn."

"How about manifestations?"

"Not me. I saw nothing. Not then. But Marianna . . . she was haunted by something she called the Smokey Man. I think I saw it outside the hospital ward. Wraithlike, insubstantial, but definitely humanoid."

Ellen smiled thinly. "That's it. That's a Watcher. Your daughter must have a talent or two you weren't aware of. It probably studied you all, but only she could see it. A natural psychic. That helps. That will help." When Brady just stared at her, she added, "In the search, Dan. It'll help the search."

In the lounge, the phone rang. It was the first phone call since Brady had returned, and it made him jump. He stared at the kitchen door for a moment, then walked quickly through the hallway, Ellen following him.

Alison? It couldn't be, could it? A ransom demand? The police?

He pushed into the lounge and didn't bother to turn on the light. It wasn't so dark, yet, that he couldn't see his way across to the phone. Ellen walked in behind him. There was a peculiar smell in the room, and it was cold. She noticed that the French windows were open.

"Did you open these?" she said, walking across to close them. Brady had snatched up the phone, and after a moment he said to Ellen, "It's Andrew. Andrew Haddingham."

"Did you open these windows?" Ellen repeated, looking towards him.

"No," he said, and then froze as he saw the look on Ellen's face. Her eyes were wide, her mouth open. She was staring beyond him, and a moment later she gave a short, stifled scream.

Brady whipped round, slamming the phone back towards the cradle, but missing. What he saw was standing there, its arm reaching out for him, made him back away in terror, crying an obscenity.

It was a man, burned from head to foot, and still clad in the charred, tattered rags of its clothing. It took a step towards Brady and its mouth opened, to show grey teeth and a pinkish tongue. The eye sockets were hollow, half concealed by the brittle, blackened lids.

Brady ran to the fire-place and drew a heavy poker from its stand. Turning back into the room he advanced upon the shambling corpse. He was white and afraid, and his heart was racing. He saw foam bubbling from the silently open mouth of the creature, but he was more aware of the hand, still reaching towards him.

"Dan! No!" cried Ellen suddenly, and Brady froze, the poker raised above his head as he moved in to the attack.

"Why the hell not? At least I can *see* this thing. Christ, what *is* it?"

Ellen had stepped towards the burned man, waving Brady back. She peered hard at the charred face. "Oh my God," she whispered. "Dan, it's Jack Baron . . . I'm sure of it. Jack Baron. The private investigator. God, how horrible!"

Fire suddenly erupted from the figure's mouth, a great jet of flame that licked towards Brady causing him to back away. The fire died down, then welled up again, appearing in the eye-sockets too, licking out, covering the blackened head in a halo of yellow light. As the fire burned in the creature's mouth, so Brady thought he heard a whining voice, a distant sound, emitted by the apparition.

He stood there in that eerie dusk, watching the burning head before him, aware of Ellen, her face yellow-bright with sweat and wonder. She walked slowly around the motionless corpse of Jack Baron. "It's speaking," she said, her voice hardly more than a whisper. She reached out towards the silent fire and Brady frowned as he saw her passing her hand through the flame. She jerked her fingers away suddenly, shaking her hand. "It's hot, but it's not real burning."

"Is he alive? Could he possibly be alive?"

Ellen shrugged, but kept her gaze on the charred body of the man she had once hired to help her. "I don't think he is. Something is animating him. The body is possessed . . ."

And as she said the words aloud, so the fire-drenched head turned to regard her. The whining voice deepened suddenly, and Brady, by listening with all his attention, could hear the word.

It was something like "TAAN," an eerie, drawn-out sound, repeated three times before the flames died from the lips and eyes and the burned figure collapsed forward onto the carpet, buckling at waist and knee.

Ellen knelt beside the body, reached out to touch the scorched head with one tentative forefinger. "What did it say?" said Brady, and for just a second Ellen shook her head, puzzled . . . sensing something, but not sure exactly what . . .

And it was as her face brightened, and she looked up at Brady, a half smile of realization on her lips, that Brady began to feel dizzy, becoming aware of a shadow moving swiftly around the room.

Ellen said, "Of course! *Dan*! It was saying *Dan*! Your name! It's you, Dan, a part of you . . ."

The words registered, but Brady could not respond to them.

He was aware only of the darting presence of a ghost, a warm, breezy presence that swirled about the room and seemed to blow stale breath into his face. Ellen's earnest features became a pale moon, an intangible reflection of something light in the whirling darkness. The wind caught Brady's hair; it jostled him, ruffled his clothing, urged him back against the wall and seemed to blow straight at him, beginning to moan and whine like a storm-wind, twisting his head this way and that. He tried to speak, but as his mouth opened so the invisible fingers snagged his tongue, and the warm, stifling wind penetrated his throat and his lungs, making his chest swell up . . .

I can't breathe, he thought through the confusion of darkness and the almost deafening wail of the storm . . .

And he heard words, Ellen's words: Don't fight it, Dan. Let it come back to you . . .

But I can't breathe, I can't breathe!

The blood thumped through his vessels; the pain in his chest increased until he felt he would burst; the stink in his nostrils grew stronger until he was sure he would start to vomit.

Out of the sensory storm, out of the darkness, the ghostly figure of a man appeared; it seemed to well up in front of him, and move towards him and into him, vanishing from sight. A face that he recognized well enough, a hollow, haunted face, certainly, with deep set, dark eyes, and the mouth open and drawn back into a corpse-like smile. And yet he recognized that face instantly.

Himself!

There were images: of his daughter, of Alison, of Rosemary, of dark figures, of burning. The images were brief, but clear and concise; they were as sharp as pictures on a screen, and they flashed chaotically before his mind's eye. His head hit the wall hard. His bursting lungs collapsed, and the breath fairly stormed from his body; he gasped for air, leaning forward, hands on his knees, and the room grew light again. He felt reassuring hands on his arms, and a woman's voice saying, "Keep breathing, Dan. Keep leaning forward. Just breathe, just take it easy."

And after a few moments he was able to straighten up again, and could see that everything in the room was calm, and bright. And without realizing that he was doing it he hugged Ellen Bancroft to his body, scarcely aware that she had responded in kind, just mercifully glad of this most human of physical contacts.

TEN

ELLEN STARED ANXIOUSLY up at Brady. "How do you feel?"

"Bloody exhausted." He was still shaking.

"I'm not surprised. Sit down for a few minutes."

Brady collapsed into one of the armchairs, stretched out his legs and stared at the ceiling. Ellen walked quickly across to the phone and placed it back on the receiver. She stepped gingerly around the corpse of Jack Baron, staring down at it, perhaps in pity, perhaps concerned with the thought of the inevitable police investigation.

Sitting down opposite Brady, she leaned forward on her knees, hands clasped. Her hair was disordered, her eyes wide and bright. She was excited, eager to convey to Brady what had occurred.

"Amazing," she said. "Quite amazing."

"That I'm exhausted? It's been a long day, what d'you expect."

"I'd expect nothing else. It's certainly amazing that you're not unconscious. But I'm more impressed by your talent. You'll have to train that talent, Dan. It could be a precious asset to you."

"Talent? Asset?" Brady was wearily regarded the woman. "That was me, right? That much I've got." He frowned, then. He was recollecting that night, three months ago. "I left my body," he said slowly. I slipped out of my body. Christ almighty, it all comes back." He straightened up in his chair.

"An OOB experience! I remember fighting the thing that was killing me. I wrestled with it. I was watching myself being strangled!"

Ellen could hardly believe what she was hearing. And what she heard delighted her. She went to the drinks cabinet. "Under the circumstances, Dan, I think you can risk a drink. You certainly need one. Gin? Scotch?"

"Brandy. What circumstances, Ellen? I don't want to be like Michael . . ."

"You're not like Michael," she said quietly, not looking at him as she poured Courvoisier into a whiskey glass. "You're strong." She brought the drink over and Brady accepted it gratefully. Strangely, as he sipped the brandy he found it less to his taste than he'd remembered. The alcohol stung; the taste was sour; the effect in his stomach was less than warming. He placed the glass down beside him.

Ellen said, "Right now, psychically you're as strong as an ox. If the thought-form appeared and attacked you, I do believe you could destroy it. You're strong, Dan. When it attacked you you recognized that the only way to defend was to attack it on a psychic level . . ."

"I thought no such thing," he cut in. "I don't think I thought at all . . ."

"Part of you did. A part of you with the talent. It saved your life. You saved your own life. You left the material, physical plane, and attacked the Stalker on its own terms. Part of you never returned."

Brady nodded his understanding. "It stayed in the house. Trapped in the house . . . it was me all along. Scaring Bill and Rosemary. The presence that even the police felt. Not the evil, not the Stalker. Me."

"Your brother thought he'd seen you when he came to the house that night. He saw your ghost. Quite literally. You disseminated almost immediately, into the stone. If only . . ." Ellen didn't complete her thoughtful sentence, but Brady prompted her. She said, "If only you could do it to order."

"Wouldn't it diminish my spirit? Wouldn't it weaken me?"

"Yes it would. You become very vulnerable. But it would strengthen the house. I'd wondered why my simple, almost token defences here were so effective. I'd felt quite safe. The

Stalker, I'm sure, was in the area, targeted on me, but it didn't properly come into the house. You were defending it."

Brady turned to peer at the blackened body in the middle of the carpet. Baron's arms were outstretched, and the charred head was covered by a towel. Brady was glad of that. "Obviously," he said. "And defending a little too effectively."

But Ellen shook her head. "Certainly you attacked Baron. But there was a reason for it. You knew you were coming home . . ."

Brady hesitated only briefly before he grasped her meaning. "And I wanted to *literally* come home! To this!" He slapped his chest.

Ellen agreed. "You possessed Baron in the only way possible. It was necessary to destroy him first, and inhabit the corpse. It's horrible, but I've read of that before. I can only take an educated guess, but I'd say the attack was violent, because the energy of your ghost was violent energy: angry. It burned him. You manifested as fire, and scorched his body even as you entered it. It was then just a question of waiting until you returned and letting the energy flow from corpse to you."

Brady stared at the body.

Ellen said, "This house will become increasingly dangerous, now. In two or three days it will be totally unsafe. We have to *make* it safe. We're going to need help. Your brother, for a start."

"My brother-in-law," Brady corrected, and added, "I can't imagine him coming back here. He was very frightened."

"He'll have to. We need help to build the wall *all* round the house. We need certain things constructed out of wood and metal. If we're to defend this house properly, Dan, if we're to make it a haven for you, for me, for anyone who comes under attack, then there's got to be a lot of heavy work. It isn't all herbs and talismans, although we'll need those too. We have to locate the source of power in the garden. We have to make trap-zones, maze-zones and sites of reflection. When psychic attack is undertaken it can be in many forms. We have to protect this house against all possibilities. We'll need help . . ."

"But Bill and Rosemary. I'm not sure . . ."

"We *need* them. For the moment. And Andrew too. We

can't *trust* anyone else, Dan. Believe me, I've been through this. I know what I'm talking about.''

"All right. I'll speak to Bill. As soon as I've been to see Andrew.''

He looked out into the garden, then laughed ironically.

"What is it?''

"I was just thinking about what you said—maze-zones, trap-zones . . . Dominick used to set traps for a Man-in-the-Oak, over there.'' He glanced at Ellen and smiled. "We called him Willie Crinkleleaf.''

"What sort of traps?''

"Herbs. Metal. Bits of mirror. Marianna used to give him hell if she caught him.''

Ellen nodded thoughtfully, amused, yet also concerned for Brady. "And where did he learn this occult practice? Not at Hillingvale . . .''

"Probably at school. The library. He'd probably cope with this better than I can!''

Ellen sighed, then stared across at the body of Jack Baron. "We have a problem. We can't just leave him here.''

Brady said quickly, "*I* have the problem, Ellen. I don't see the point of your being involved in this.'' He stooped and drew Baron's limbs into the body, straightening the corpse. Checking his hands he found that very little of the charred clothing had rubbed off onto his skin. "Did you see a car outside?'' he asked, and Ellen said. "Yes. Tucked away into the trees, down the road a way. It had darkened windows.''

"I saw it too. Baron's for sure, and with luck the police won't have noticed it yet. Baron was burned in this room, but he certainly came in again from outside, so let's get him back there. You take the legs.''

Ellen bent to the task. Baron's corpse was heavy, and she staggered slightly as Brady backed towards the French windows. He led the way out across the lawns, to the hidden places beyond the elms. They placed the body in the wood and leaf-litter that the children had helped pile against the wall, the previous autumn.

"In a day or so I'll get the police round.''

"And tell them what?''

"What's to tell? I came home. I found the burned patch but

thought little of it. A day or so later I was checking round the garden and found the body."

They stood in the gloom below the trees, only just able to make out each other's features. It was cold, and Ellen shivered. She said, "Baron was a street boy, from the East End. He was half bad himself and a gangland killing isn't beyond reason . . ."

"Leaving the corpse at the site of his latest investigation? Yes, I can see a certain amount of like-thinking among the Thames police. The important thing is, *I* didn't do it, and I've been in hospital for months. The police might ask a lot of questions, but there's no need to tell them about reanimation, or possession . . . and there's no need for you to be involved at all."

"Thank you."

"For what?"

"For considering me."

"I'm considering us both," said Brady. "The fewer complications that get in the way of what I have to do the better. Dumb is the best policy, and that's how I intend to play it. But if you—one of Baron's clients—just happened to be here when the body was discovered, then I can see a more rigorous and repetitive line of questioning coming our way. Go home, Ellen. For the moment."

They walked quickly back to the house and exchanged telephone numbers. Ellen said, "This house will not be safe for long. And nor will you."

"I know. But we *will* make it safe."

Her stare was a searching one. "Then you want me to come back?"

Brady reached out and took her hands between his. He smiled as he said, "With one exception I can't think of anything that I'd like more at the moment. If I'm as strong as you say, then that strength can work for the both of us. But I thank God for you, Ellen, for the hope you bring me."

She reached out and pinched his cheek. "Stick with it, Dan," she said, before walking briskly out of the house, heading for the station.

— ELEVEN ————————————

IT WAS DAN BRADY who had answered the phone, Andrew Haddingham was sure of that. The voice had been subdued, yet unmistakably Dan. But that brief contact had been abruptly broken: Haddingham had heard a woman's voice, and a startled cry, and then the line had gone dead. When he had tried ringing back, the line had been engaged.

He stood for several seconds staring at the black phone, thinking hard. The woman's voice, yes, he had recognized that too. Ellen Bancroft. She had made contact with Brady at last, then.

But that cry. And the abrupt cutting off of the open line. Ellen had told him that he should never, under any circumstances, contact the police if he believed her to be in trouble. He was well used to Ellen's ghostly encounters, and the moments of intense fear that would continue to haunt her life for many months. What had happened at Brook's Corner he couldn't imagine—or rather, he could! He felt helpless, though. He would have to believe that whatever had startled the two of them could be controlled, or repelled.

It was a belief not hard to accept. Ellen had proved adept at doing just that, over the past months.

Haddingham tried the number once more. It was still engaged. Behind him, the door to his small office opened and George Campbell's florid face stared at him quizzically. "Come on, Andrew. We're closing the meeting."

Haddingham picked up his red folder and followed the Director down the short corridor to the briefing room at the end.

Every six months the teams from the Ennean Institute of Paranormal Research and Hillingvale met to share knowledge, findings and exchange ideas. This was the fourth and final session of the day.

Campbell was in the chair, of course, his briar pipe placed carefully to his left, his folder opened in the middle, a green phone to his right. The younger team members had left earlier in the afternoon. Only Elizabeth Smallwood, the Ennean Institute's Director, was left.

Professor Smallwood was a po-faced woman in her early fifties; but by tugging her grey hair back into a tight bun, and refusing all forms of make-up, dental care, or clothes consciousness, she had contrived to pass for sixty, and gave the impression of living in the nineteen-forties. Andrew Haddingham disliked her intensely, and found her hard to cope with, especially since Ellen Bancroft had left the team: Ellen had managed to mediate well between the two of them. Smallwood had an abrasive way of talking, and her steel-eyed gaze could fix on a body and remain there unwaveringly as she challenged, or cross-questioned, or criticized. Haddingham found her very threatening.

She had done a considerable amount of all three today, as the weaknesses in the collaborative efforts between the two outposts of paranormal research became apparent. The stringent adherence of Hillingvale to the Official Secrets Act placed strictures upon the mutual workings of the two teams that were wholly unacceptable to Professor Smallwood, and she had complained bitterly all afternoon. It was not that work *wasn't* shared, nor that information did not pass from Hillingvale to the Ennean: it did, and in great abundance. But it was clear to Smallwood that the *quality* of that information differed according to the direction of flow. From the Ennean came the best, most pertinent, and astonishing results—apportation, ectoplasm, medium-contact with the dead. From Hillingvale came dull accounts of rodents reacting psychically to danger, came boring details of crystal lattice absorption of electromagnetic energy, tedious reports on the penetration of the human aura through a variety of different material barriers.

Clearly, the Ministry of Defence was not playing fair, and was keeping back its most vital research conclusions, hidden beneath the bulk of the Official Secrets Act.

As the meeting drew towards its close, that late afternoon, Haddingham finished his idle skim of the Ennean's research file while Campbell and Professor Smallwood talked about future meetings.

A great deal of it, this time, concerned regression under deep hypnosis, and seance-contact. There were pages and pages of incoherent ramblings, accounts of past lives, and messages from the Otherworld. There were samples of psychic writing, two sheafs of psychic music, the inevitable telekinetic studies, and the Ennean's speciality: apportation. Haddingham scrutinized the photographs of three supposed Celtic figurines very carefully. The originals—carried through time from some two thousand years before—were being examined by the British Museum. The BM were sceptical, Haddingham knew, because he had spoken to them two weeks before. It amused him to note that no record of the Museum's negative findings appeared in the committee's report.

But something in those reports had ticked Haddingham's curiosity, and set the wheels moving in his head. He couldn't pin it down exactly, but the nagging thought grew on him as he turned the pages, flipping back through the file, trying to identify what exactly it *was* that had registered on him subconsciously.

It was as the meeting was finally declared closed (Professor Smallwood's abrasive tone stating, "And a very unsatisfactory meeting, George. You really *will* have to understand that.") that Haddingham felt the blood drain from his face, and found his vision swimming slightly, the dizzying response to that minor shock that is sudden realization.

It was not something he had read in this most *recent* set of reports that had been crying out for attention, it was a series of short work notes from the *last* meeting, and perhaps from the meetings before that!

Campbell's voice broke through his thoughts. "Are you all right, Andrew?"

Haddingham glanced up. The Director was regarding him curiously, his pale eyes glittering. Professor Smallwood had left. Haddingham stood, closing the folder, and smiled. "Yes. Why do you ask? I was just absorbed in all this nonsense. It does me good to be reminded that the lunatic fringe is still flourishing."

Campbell glanced through his own folder of copied sheets. "Some very tedious reading here, I grant you. Can't say I read their last report through, not in its entirety."

"I did," said Haddingham softly. "Just once. And very quickly. But I read it through."

And thank God I did, he thought. *Thank God I was conscientious. Otherwise I might have missed it. It might not have registered.*

He hastened to his small office, and went straight to the file marked "miscellaneous."

There were three previous reports from the Ennean Institute, the earliest dated nearly eighteen months before, and quite thin. Haddingham could remember nothing about any of its contents as he quickly flipped through the closely typed pages.

But buried in the whole mass of paperwork were a number of brief references whose true importance was just beginning to register upon him. Refusing to be forgotten, only now did they start to fidget for his attention.

He drove straight home and placed a frozen pizza, and some oven-chips into the small stove. Then he tried Brady's number again, and this time—to his delight—got through to the man.

They arranged for Brady to come over at about nine o'clock.

Haddingham lived spartanly in his two-bedroomed apartment, on the ground floor of an elegant Georgian house that had been converted to flats some years before. He could never be bothered to cook properly, depending on the excuse of company, female companions, and vitamins to induce the correct mineral and dietary balance in his far-from-frail physique.

Now, as the pizza heated through, he went straight to the lounge, turned on all the lights, and placed the great wad of reports onto the coffee table in front of the sofa. He placed

soft music onto the Hitachi—Brahms—and poured himself
half a glass of scotch, before deciding against it, and tipping
the spirit back into the bottle.

He checked his pulse, looked at his tongue in the mirror,
and breathed deeply several times. He felt a little dizzy, and as
he walked about the room he felt distinctly ill at ease.

Quickly then, deciding to take no chances, he placed small
iron bowls of dilute nitric acid at the four corners of the
lounge. Into each he sprinkled a little salt, from a linen bag on
which was marked a Christian seal. He went upstairs and
stripped totally naked, standing under the shower for a few
minutes, then dressed in meticulously cleaned white slacks and
a white, linen shirt.

His sense of unease faded. Although it was almost certainly
auto-suggestion, with two of his friends undergoing psychic
attack it made sense to be cautious.

The smell of the acid in the lounge was sharp, but when he
burned sweet herbs in a copper dish, the room took on a cosy,
homely feel. He fetched the pizza and chips, and a fork, and
began to absently feed on them as he turned the pages of the
three reports, seeking the information that he had subconsciously registered months before.

It was an hour before he found the first piece he sought.

It was a sample of psychic writing from a seventeen-year old
youth who slipped, almost without control, into trance conditions, and produced as near-perfect a facsimile of seventeenth
century English handwriting as any expert had ever seen. To
produce the untidy, spidery script the boy had used his left
hand, although he was normally right-handed. The samples
consisted, for the most part, of obscure symbols, nonsense
words, some of which proved to be anagrams, and incoherent babble. There were moments of lucid prose, but these
amounted to apparently arcane references, passages of de-
scription, and requests for understanding, presented in a
pleading, almost begging tone.

Academics at Cambridge who had examined the writing had
stated that, although the work was clearly fakery, had they
been genuine they would evince some knowledge of alchemy,
and the mystic arts of the time of the philosopher Robert
Fludd, and others. In fact, there was an awesome reflection of

Fludd's own handwriting in the cryptic style that the youth
produced, but no verbal or written clue as to the "name" of
the psychic contact had ever emerged. What drew Haddingham's attention, now, was the passage that he had noticed before. Written over a year ago, it read simply:

"He is awakening, and that awakening is of the first order.
Now they will gather and the eyes of the lazarine will open. A
RACH NIAR. Rocas. Oh Void, the Awakening, Rotor
Rotas."

Haddingham removed that particular sheet, and used a pencil to ring the short, typed phrase. To his irritation the original
—or a copy of the original—had not been included with the
report.

In the margin he scribbled: Lazarine = lazarus? A RACH
NIAR = Arachne? Rotor/Rotas = wheel, or turning. Fate?

He moved on quickly, however, since the main piece he
wished to relocate was deeper in the file. He found it at last,
and sat back, his skin cold, his heart beating hard as he read
through the short exchange between a medium and a ques-
tioner, made some six months previous. It was not the reference to "Dan" that had made him spot the piece, at that
meeting during the summer, but the reference to The Awakening. All through the reports, from various psychic fields, he
had seen that reference, and at the time it had seemed just
another part of the Ennean's paranormal quackery.

Now he stared at those papers: at the bizzare, at the odd,
at the freak and at the lunatic; and he wondered seriously
whether the Ministry of Defence might not have been seriously
underplaying its hand, working in areas hardly removed from
realistic physics and chemistry. He wondered if his personal
commitment to the idea of metaphysics without the occult
might not have been the most serious blindness he had experienced in all his fifty-five years.

The report was titled:

*Angela Huxley: medium. Self-induced trance and seance
contact, August 27th 198—. Contact unidentified.*

8:31. Physical distress, head shaking, subdued sound of
sobbing. Contact with spirit "Harold" broken, apparently
unwillingly.

8:33. Stillness. AH staring straight ahead, sweating profusely.

8:36. New Contact. "Who can I tell?" Voice slightly
deeper than normal AH.

Q. Who are you?
"Who can I tell?"
Q. What do you wish to tell?
"Who can I tell?"
Q. Will you identify yourself? Do you have a name?
"Who can I tell?"
Q. What do you wish to tell?
"They are awakening."
Q. Who is awakening?

8:40. *Silence.* AH breathing heavily. Body shaking. Still
profusely sweating. Three full minutes silence after the last
question.

8:43. Q. Who is awakening?
"They can reach. They have reached. They are awaken-
ing."
Q. Who is this message for? Is it for anyone at this table?
"Tell him. Tell him they are awakening. Tell Dan. Tell
him."
Q. Who is Dan?
"Tell Dan. They are gathering. They have reached. Tell
him."
Q. Who is Dan?
Silence.

8:47. AH emerges from trance and is physically sick. Reports that she felt as if she had been in an ice-cold wind.

In the hour before Dan Brady arrived, Haddingham located
two more references to 'the awakening.' He was sure there
were more, but they eluded him in the dense-packed reports
and pages. His back was aching, and his eyes were sore. He sat
back in the sofa, staring at the report of the seance with
Angela Huxley, and the name 'Dan' seemed to swim in and
out of focus. Seances were riddled with names, scattered in
and among the various messages with great abundance. Why
was he so certain that *this* Dan was meant to be Daniel Brady?
On August 27th, if he remembered correctly, the Bradys had

been in Holland, a happily complete family, holidaying in Amsterdam.

It would be four months before the tragedy struck. Why should a spirit wish to communicate with Dan with what sounded like a warning?

Unless the spirit "knew" at that time that Brady was being targeted? Brady had certainly complained of tiredness and headaches over the summer. Haddingham had thought nothing of it. Psychic attack was the last thing he had on his mind.

It would not be for a month that Ellen Bancroft would be so brutally attacked and he would find himself drawn into her truly bizarre world of occult power, and directional evil. And by that time his brief, inadequate perusal of the reports from the Ennean Institute would have been forgotten.

Awakening. Gathering. Reaching. Targeting. It added up to practically nothing. Except for gathering. He could understand that. Ellen had said she had sensed that her attackers were gathering. Would Dan Brady have had the same experience?

Brady turned up just before nine o'clock, and he and Haddingham greeted each other like the old friends they were—with one exception: they left the drinks firmly locked away in the cabinet.

They talked briefly, and grimly, about what had happened three months ago, and Brady explained how, with Ellen's help, he was going to turn Brook's Corner into a sort of psychic fortress. Haddingham listened silently, and without expression. He was slightly shocked by Brady's changed appearance. Brady had always been a full-figured, rather indulged looking man. Now he was grey-eyed and gaunt, his handsome face chiselled, the pale skin darkened with a couple of days' growth of beard that he hadn't bothered to shave off. Although his hands shook as he held the papers that Haddingham wanted him to read, there was an unfamiliar strength about the younger man, an ice-cold hardness—the eyes were haunted, but now they saw *everything*; the lips were parted in a half smile, but it was a disarming smile, an expression that Haddingham believed could touch a man's face in the moments before he cold-bloodedly killed.

Brady finished reading and they talked some more, Brady making it clear that he was finished with the Ministry, and with work of any kind, until he had hunted down the attackers of his family.

"What will you do for money? Have you thought of that?"

"I have savings. I have all of Alison's money, and she was well off . . ."

"Inherited money. Yes."

"And several books she wrote under her maiden name. She made a small fortune. My father too. He'll help. And I'll try and get what I can out of the Government. Ideally they'll let me stay on the payroll . . . as a field worker."

"I can't see it," said Haddingham.

"Nor me. But I'll try. Savings won't last forever, especially if I pay off the mortgage."

"I'll do what I can," said Haddingham, impressed by the way Brady was beginning to think clearly, shaking off the initial shock and sadness that had followed his recovery. "The stumbling block will be George Campbell. He was never very keen on you. I can't see him writing a recommendation for sabbatical leave."

"Damn Campbell. I was never establishment enough for him." Brady rubbed his eyes. He was tired and the smell of burning herbs was irritating them. "Mandrake?" he asked with a smile. "Hemlock?"

"Garlic, hellbore root, and simple fragrances. I've got an elementary block up around the room, just nitric acid and consecrated salt. Ellen's idea. I can't say it *doesn't* work, because I don't know if I've been targeted. But it's comforting."

Brady shook his head, almost in disbelief. He looked around the cosily lit room, at the elegant furniture, at the huge colour TV, with its video recorder tucked neatly away below, at the beautiful picture of earthrise over the moon's surface, which had been Haddingham's favourite image from the early seventies. And he looked at four iron dishes at the corners of the room, and the tiny copper brazier with its thin trail of incense smoke rising into the air. "It's a new world, Andrew. For all my working with supernature, I could never have imagined this . . ."

"I know what you mean."

"Talking to Ellen today," Brady went on, "made me feel like I was insane. Some of the things she said should have made me laugh. With derision. Instead, I took it all in. I've come to accept it, to believe it. Root extracts, burned herbs, metal bracelets, talismans, seals, markings in the air . . . defences against mind power that my common sense says can't possibly work."

"I know *exactly* what you mean," Haddingham repeated, re-experiencing this own difficulty in acceptance.

Brady said, "But something killed three people at the hospital, on my ward. And that something tried to kill me. And it couldn't get me. I was defended. It's madness. And perhaps for the rest of my life I have to be a part of that madness."

For a moment Haddingham just stared at his colleague. Then he smiled. "It's odd, isn't it? Both you and I work in the field of the paranormal. Physicists laugh at us; the scientific community spurns us, despite the fact that we are 'establishment;' the police are sceptical even when they can actually see results like psychic body location. But we're just as bad. I never though that beyond simple supernature there might be a real, occult world of spirits, witches, religious phenomena, Hermetic correspondences, representational magic. It's the way we were trained. Rational training for rational minds, with the emphasis on rationality."

As if the words were triggering some uncomfortable associations in his head, Brady licked his lips and laughed nervously. "Quite. It takes some adjusting to."

"You've adjusted well. Your own words, Dan. But for me, it's taken time. Even when Ellen's family were taken, even when the Stalker began to attack her, I couldn't really believe everything she said. It took the destruction of your family . . . it took Alison's disappearance, and those hideous wounds on your body, to start the ball rolling in *my* head. To start me believing."

Leaning forward in his seat, Haddingham picked up the few sheets of paper he had marked out from the files. Staring at them he said, "I feel lost, Dan. I feel totally lost. What in God's name are we up against?"

"That," said Brady, "is what I intend to find out." He took the papers from Haddingham and there was a silence as

he skimmed them again, shaking his head. At last he said,
"It's a big jump from 'Tell Dan' to 'Tell Daniel Brady of
Brook's Corner.' I'm not sure, Andrew. It could have been a
message for anybody."

But Haddingham disagreed. "I don't think so. Don't ask
me why. Don't ask me to be rational. It's you, it was meant
for you. We can set up a seance with the same medium, if you
like. Try and get the same spirit back."

" 'They are awakening,' " Brady read from the sheets.
" '*He* is awakening. *They* are awakening. Tell Dan. They are
reaching. Lazarus, Arachne, Wheels of Fate.' " He glanced at
Haddingham. "Something is beginning, then. It's been beginning for a year or so. An awakening, followed by a gathering.
Alison was gathered. And Marianna, and Dom. And before
them, Michael Bancroft and Ellen's boy. And before them . . .
others. Sutherland said there had been two other incidents like
mine. Perhaps there have been more . . . in other countries. Or
disappearances that have never been reported, or which seem
to be different from the disappearance of Alison." He looked
down again. "Awakening. Gathering. But for what purpose,
Andrew? For what purpose?"

"God knows!" Haddingham's face was pale. The room
seemed cold.

"I wonder if they're alive . . ." Brady's voice had dropped.
The hard edge had dulled for a moment, and it was a dejected,
shattered man who sat across the table.

"Who can tell? Don't think about it—" Stupid words!
Haddingham felt immediately angry with himself.

Brady looked up sharply and there were tears in his eyes. "I
think about it all the time! I can't accept that they're dead.
They *must* be alive. But for how long? Why were they gathered? *For what purpose*?" He lowered his gaze, his head shaking.

For a moment Haddingham thought that Dan Brady would
weep. He said nothing, just watched and waited for the sudden tension in his friend to drain away. At last Brady looked
up, and his eyes glittered between the narrowed lids. The
animal was back. The killer was in control again.

Haddingham said, "They're powerful, Dan. Christ knows,
they're powerful. To be able to attack you and Ellen in the

way they're attacking . . . whoever they are, they're years ahead of us when it comes to mind power. We're grubbing around at the edges of abilities that these people . . . or whatever they are . . . can use with facility. They're strong, Dan. They're awesomely strong."

Brady placed the reports back on the coffee table, and clenched his fingers before him, staring at Haddingham as he let the man's words sink in. "I agree," he said, his voice becoming soft, the tone almost deadly. "But they have weaknesses, Andrew. Ellen has told me that. They are strong, but I am strong also. They are *gathering*. Perhaps they are spread thin, therefore. But I am hunting. I don't spread my strength. And the nearer I get to them, the stronger I shall become."

After a moment: "And where will you begin? Your hunt?"

"Right here. Where else? I have only one contact . . ."

"The thought-form."

"Precisely. The beast that stalks me. There is a mind behind that beast; and there is a man around the mind. And he's one of them. The first of them. Ellen thinks she can get to know who it is. The moment she finds out I shall find him, and I shall kill him. I shall stalk him as he has stalked me. And the weapon that he is using, the violent force of his mind, is the way I shall find him."

"How?"

"By snaring it. By trapping it. By capturing it at Brook's Corner. Ellen thinks it's possible. If we can trap the beast, we can immobilize the man who has created it." Brady smiled, but there was no warmth in that gesture, rather a sense of anticipated triumph. "It's a beginning. The end may take months to reach, but I shall hunt them all down. And I shall find my family again, of that I swear. I shall *die* before I cease to search for them."

The quiet passion, and the gently voiced anger with which Brady had spoken, subdued Haddingham for a moment. Again, he was impressed by the way the young man seemed to have transformed from being soft and easy going into something hard, something with a cutting edge. The lean, hollow features, the deep, dark-rimmed eyes, belonged on another man, a crueller man, a colder man than Daniel Brady.

"What can *I* do for you, Dan?"

"You've done something already." Brady nodded towards the files. "These. It's something to add to what I have already . . . an amulet like a severed head; the names Wickhurst and Magondathog; a jewelled object; and a man with a face like a corpse. Maybe something else will turn up. Watch and listen, Andrew. At the Ministry and at the Ennean. It surely can't be a coincidence that of three families struck by this terror . . . three families *collected* . . . that two surviving members worked in the field of the paranormal."

With a shrug of his shoulders, Haddingham at once agreed to listen and watch at Hillingvale, but also struck a negative note. "The police interviewed me, and several people in the department. But I don't think they make a connection. Their theory—"

"*Is* coincidence. I know. I've spoken to them too."

"The first family to be . . . collected . . . they were ordinary. What I mean is, no connections with occult work at all. They left a child and a mother, who didn't work, took the father, who was a college lecturer, and two children." He hesitated. "But Dan . . ."

Brady knew what was coming. Haddingham said softly, "They *killed* those they didn't take. It's the *pattern* of the attack that gives the connection. But you . . . you and Ellen . . . you both survived. Why the hell was that?"

"Strength," said Brady, enigmatically from Haddingham's point of view. "And weakness. Two bad mistakes." Brady was smiling, that same smile of bitter triumph.

Haddingham shivered as he regarded the man, not particularly liking this ice-cold manifestation of his old friend.

He said quietly, "And so the hunt begins."

— TWELVE

BECAUSE THE TALK had gone on well past midnight, Brady ended up staying the night at Haddingham's flat. He awoke at six, alert and clear-headed. He got up immediately, made himself coffee, then drove home.

At eight o'clock sharp Bill Suchock turned up, and Brady told him what he required: an extension of the eight-foot wall that bounded part of the grounds of the house. An extension to completely enclose Brook's Corner.

Suchock looked tired and slightly crumpled. It was concern for Rosemary, of course, and concern, too, for his brother-in-law. Since Brady had come out of his coma, there had been a tension in the Suchock household and a heavy, at time unbearable, silence. It was as if they were haunted, as if something were eroding them. Suchock could put it down only to concern for the experiences they had had at Brook's Corner over the last few months, and the fear of returning there ever again.

This much he had said to Brady on the phone the previous night, almost by way of an apology. But Brady had already detected the heavy cloud of apprehension and unease in the Suchock household, and no explanations were necessary. Rosemary was generating a guilt-laden anxiety, and it was eating into everything, into Bill, into Malcolm, everything . . .

They walked the periphery of the grounds, past the ruined chicken coops, the stands of fruit trees, the low fence that overlooked woodland. There was a lot of building involved, and it would cost Dan Brady several thousand pounds, and a labor force of perhaps five men.

Brady had the money.

Suchock stood and stared at the wall, shaking his head. Then he glanced at Brady. "Good God," he said. "I think you're mad. All this to stop being attacked again. But if it's what you want . . . personally I'd have bought two shotguns, and half a dozen dogs."

With a wry laugh, Brady said, "Shotguns? I'm getting those too." How could he say to Suchock that not everything which would be coming against him would be tangible enough to be stopped with lead shot, nor by a wall. The wall was the beginning. Brick was better than wood, though stone would have been best. The important thing, for Brady, was the feeling of security. And for Ellen Bancroft, the fact that things could be built effectively *into* walls, and not smashed out: things like symbols, seals, metal talismans, defences of a sort that no man would think of as defences, but which could throw a shadow wall up against such violent elementals as would be coming for the occupants of Brook's Corner.

At nine o'clock, Brady called the police. He first covered the burned carpet in the lounge with a sofa, hoping to avoid the more awkward questions.

Two uniformed constables arrived first, by car. They said very little to Brady. They looked at the body, walked around the garden, checked the other side of the wall. They opened the doors to Baron's car, as soon as their attention had been directed to it by Brady himself. They asked him simple questions: how he had found the body, when he had last walked in that part of the garden. The moment he told them that he had been in hospital for some months they realized who he was, and seemed stuck for anything further to say.

Sutherland arrived a few minutes later, with a youthful, sour-faced assistant, who stood and walked around (even sat) with his hands clasped in front of him. Sutherland crouched to study the body, and watched as the police doctor, who arrived almost at the same time as the CID, made a more thorough examination.

"I've not seen anything like this, before," the doctor said, rising to his feet and packing away his equipment. He glanced at Sutherland. "Have you?"

"Not so charred."

"Unusual burning. I'm tempted to say he's not been dead more than a couple of days. But I'm afraid everything depends on the autopsy. I've got all I need here, thanks."

Photographers, forensic men, youthful policemen in plain clothes scouring the garden in the area of the wall . . . the process seemed to take forever. Brady became uncomfortable watching it all. The police looked in the lounge almost cursorily. They saw that the French windows had been forced. Brady admitted that they'd been like that when he came home.

"Did you notice the car when you came home?"

"Yes I did. I didn't think anything of it."

The phone went. It was for Sutherland. After a minute or two he came back to Brady. "The car belonged to a man called John Henry Baron. Jack Baron. Name mean anything to you? That's almost certainly Baron out there."

"Means nothing," said Brady.

Sutherland stared at him, almost quizzically. "Odd," he said.

"Odd?"

"You lose your family horribly. You are savagely attacked. You spend three months in a coma. While you are in hospital a 'maniac' kills two nurses, one of them most disgustingly, and one patient. You come out of hospital and there's a grotesquely burned man in your garden. What the hell are you, Mister Brady? A walking Nemesis?"

He glanced down at the notes he had taken on the phone. "The man Baron has quite a record. A lot of time . . . assault, robbery, racketeering. Not your most salubrious of men. He's a registered PD. Private Detective. That's odd too." Staring at Brady. The policeman's face was white, severe. The grey eyes glittered. His young colleague stood by the door, watching and waiting, and Brady was convinced that at a signal from Sutherland he would come across and start using his fists. Quite happily.

But Sutherland just said, "A dead PD found in the garden of a man whose family have disappeared. A disappearance that is baffling the police. Just the sort of case, in fact, where a

PD might be employed to help. Mister Brady, my credibility is
being stretched to painful limits.''

Brady kept his cool, despite a nagging feeling of uncertainty
that his dumb play was necessarily the best thing. But he
knew, for sure, that he needed the house defended, and fast;
and any sort of repeated police presence might put obstacles in
the way of that defence.

For the moment he wanted nothing to do with such babysit-
ting.

He said, ''I've told you what happened, Inspector Sutherland. I can tell you no more than I know. A deserted garden
seems a good place to put a body to me. That's all I can suggest.''

''We'll take prints from the house, just to see if he came in.
You don't mind?''

''Not at all.''

''We'll need prints from you, from anyone and everyone
who's been in the house in the last three months, purely for
elimination purposes you understand. Strange prints will
stand out, that way.''

Damn!

''And we'll leave a man with you, if you like . . .''

''Not necessary. Thanks all the same.''

Sutherland frowned. ''Aren't you afraid that the men who
attacked you might come back?''

''Why should they? They got what they wanted.''

Sutherland almost laughed, staring at Brady most curiously.
''I can't make up my mind, Mister Brady, whether your re-
sponses are cooperative or uncooperative. I'm trying to help
you. We're doing all we can to help. We'll continue to search
for your wife and children, believe me. But you *must* cooperate. If you hold anything back, anything at all, it might deny
us the chance to make a link . . . do you understand me?''

''Yes I do, Inspector. I understand you very well. And you
must understand *me*. I am cooperating, and I shall continue to
cooperate. What happened to my family has left me wounded,
and bitter, and quite, *quite* determined!'' He leaned forward
in his seat, trying to summon the same intensity for Sutherland
as the policeman himself had displayed. ''I'm determined to
find them! I don't want a police presence because I'd *welcome*

the return of those who attacked me. Can't you see that? I *want* them to come again. I *want* them to come and try to finish what they started. I am going to defend this house, and myself."

"You are going to take the law into your own hands . . ." cut in Sutherland grimly. He shook his head, but before he could add anything, Brady said, "No. I'm not. I said I'd co-operate and I meant it. I'll maintain close links with you. I'll keep you informed of everything I find out. But right now, I know nothing. If I invite attack, I stand a chance of under-standing a little more of what happened here. I *must* know if my family is still alive."

For a second Sutherland considered that, then he leaned back in his chair and sighed. And nodded. "It makes a sort of sense. We'll keep a police presence in the area, then. There will always be a patrol car within minutes of you. And we *will* watch you, and your house. We'll talk again, Mr. Brady."

By the time the forensic squad had finished dusting the house for prints, and sniffing around for anything else that might have been important, it was gone two o'clock. Brady was hungry, and his stomach felt hollow, his breath stale. The chairs had not been moved in the lounge; the patch of burning re-mained undiscovered.

It was as the police were packing away their things, and politely refusing yet another coffee, that Brady felt a sudden chill. He shivered. An icy sweat broke out on his body and face, and he quickly wiped a towel across his cheeks and fore-head. His heart had started to hammer in his chest, and the room swam before his eyes. He felt quite disorientated, quite sick. None of the police seemed to notice, and they left by the front door and drove noisily away.

Immediately Brady went to the kitchen and stuffed bread and cheese into his mouth, bulking up his stomach and con-suming a pint of milk to help wash the food down. Then he poured vinegar into four china saucers, sprinkled salt into each of them and made the sign of the cross above the solu-tions. He was not a Catholic, though he could claim a Chris-tian belief. But he was not convinced that his simple act would effectively consecrate the salt, so he searched for fully ten

minutes among the junk boxes upstairs in the spare room until
he found the small flask of 'blessed water' from the shrine at
Knock, in West Ireland, which the family had visited a year
and a half ago. He sprinkled several drops of this into each
saucer and then spoke magic words above them:

"For Christ's sake work, damn you!"

The saucers he placed around the lounge. Then he went to
the phone. The tension in his chest was growing, not receding.
The blood pumped in surges through his temples. He rang
Ellen Bancroft.

"I think I'm being targeted. My whole body is shaking."

"Have you eaten?"

"Yes. And I've not touched alcohol. I've got salt and
vinegar solution around the room. What else?"

"The sign I showed you. Make it to the windows and the
door to the hall. Sit in a chair, facing the window, and draw a
circle with animal fat—butter will do—around it. Believe in it,
Dan, and don't forget the star symbol, especially if you feel
something enter the house."

"Christ almighty!" Brady said, shivering and unhappy.
"Circles, pentagrams . . . bloody dracula!"

"Do it!" Ellen shouted down the line. "I'm coming to you
now. I've packed as much as I think I'll need, but I can't carry
it all, so I'm getting a taxi. I'll be there in about two hours.
Strength, Dan. Remember that. And *belief*. You're strong.
Just because you can sense yourself being targeted doesn't
mean you can be harmed . . . not just yet. Go easy."

Brady hung up, walked quickly to the kitchen and found a
pat of English butter. He almost laughed as he returned to the
lounge, closed the door, smeared the carpet around the chair
in a closed circle, then sat down.

For the true believer, Ellen had told him, *for those who
know that these defences do work, the circle is created
imaginatively, with the point of an imaginary sword. You
must learn to fight mind with mind. It is not the physical
defence that works, it is the belief behind the defence. Do
everything in a ritual, calculated way. Any action performed
with intention becomes a rite, so don't bathe just to cleanse
your body, bathe with the intention of purifying mind and
body both, and banishing all clinging evil influence.*

So Brady made the circle, and believed in it as intensely as he could, thinking through the action, imagining the potent barrier to any destructive 'psychic substance' that might come against him.

He was in the country, where elemental attack was more potent and effective; he was alone, which was something earnestly to be avoided when one was a target; his house had no running water in its vicinity, meaning that it could be attacked from all sides; and Ellen had divined the presence of some form of ancient ruin close by, which Brady thought was probably the Roman villa reputed to be buried in the area: and such ancient places were powerful foci of psychic energy, and an attacking elemental could draw upon that energy.

All things considered, he was vulnerable and breaking the prime rules of psychic self-defence. But Ellen had convinced him of his immediate safety, and of the fact that Brook's Corner would make an ideal fortress.

Nevertheless, he completed the ritual she had described to him, feeling slightly foolish, but discovering that his embarrassment faded in scant seconds: he stood facing east and made the air sign that Ellen had shown him: thumb and end two fingers folded in, index and middle finger extended. The hand drawn through the air in an inverted V, then drawn in three sweeping lines across that, the total sign being the five pointed star that could be contained in a pentagram. As he drew the sign he said aloud the words, "May the mighty archangel Raphael protect me from all evil approaching from the East." Turning to the south he repeated the sign, and invoked the archangel Michael; to the west he called upon the strength of Gabriel, and from the north, Uriel. At the end of this solemn ritual he was sweating, his right arm shaking badly.

I'm a thirty-five year old scientist, not particularly religious, and here I am asking angels for help. Christ almighty! Or is that the same thing?

Banish all doubt, Ellen had said to him. *When you summon forces for help, you are really summoning the force from your own mind. Belief in the ritual opens the way for belief in your own powers of defence.*

He sat down heavily in the chair, and waited, thinking

about what he had done. The smell of vinegar in the room was strong and unpleasant. He had erected defences against weak elemental forces that might have been in the room, or just outside. But what was coming at him was not weak. Would those defences hold?

As he sat and waited, so the tension went away. His heart slowed its beat, and his breathing became more normal.

When the taxi drew up, at three forty-five, sounding its horn twice, Brady felt confident enough to step out of the circle and out of the lounge to welcome Ellen Bancroft back.

THIRTEEN

THE FIRST TANGIBLE attack came three days later, an hour or
so before dusk. It was an overcast day, and there had been
rain earlier. The gardens were slick with wetness, and the grey,
miserable mood had infected everyone on the site, Bill Suchock especially, but his seven casual labourers too.

The wall had been extended all round the garden, and had
been built to a height of two feet, behind the existing fencing.
The work had been going on from five a.m. until late at night;
no-one was complaining about that, least of all the brick-
layers, whose promised wages were double what they could
normally have expected. Suchock had experienced little
trouble obtaining the bricks and mortar, but he was concerned
about the police car that regularly prowled along the country
road and back lane of Brook's Corner. Brady's reassurance
that the police had more important things on their minds than
whether or not planning permission had been obtained, did
nothing to decrease Bill Suchock's anxiety.

It was an anxiety, of course, that had a deeper root. He was
here, on this Saturday, working full out on bricklaying himself; but he was here despite Rosemary's protests, and against
his better judgement. He was ill-at-ease, edgy, and rather
short-tempered. When Rosemary and Malcolm came at lunch-
time, bringing a consignment of modelling clay for Ellen, the
whole family huddled in the kitchen, silently watching the
noisy workmen as they drank beer (Ellen couldn't dissuade

them from that) and ate thick-cut sandwiches. Rosemary jumped with fright every time Brady came up behind her, or asked her to do something. Her face looked more drawn than those few days ago when he had emerged from hospital. Clearly, she had not been sleeping, and she tugged at Suchock's jacket, repeatedly whispering, "Let's go, Bill. Let's go home, now."

"You don't have to come here, Rosie," Brady reassured her. "I can see that the place terrifies you, I'm not going to be upset. I can always visit you."

Rosemary, her fists clenched, her hollow eyes wide, yet very weary, smiled thinly and said, "I want to do what I can, Dan. I want to help . . . Whatever you're doing."

"You can help us best by being on call for errands. Like fetching clay. But you're not looking well, Rosie. I don't think you should come here . . ."

He was thinking, of course, that her physical and mental weakness made her far too vulnerable to attack. Ellen had hinted that any weak, spiritual presence in the house could attract destructive psychic energy, and so for all their sakes Rosemary Suchock should be discouraged from coming to Brook's Corner. Fitness was a potent defense against mind attack. Bodily fitness was paramount. All wounds had to be cleaned instantly, and left open to the air, since necrosis and suppuration—foci of decomposition—were attractive to low forms of elemental life, which could work their way into a body and take possession. Brady was under instruction to have a tooth removed, since the decay in it was advanced and an abscess might form at any time. Mentally, however, Brady was strong, his most obvious weakness being his memories of Alison and his two children, and his inability to prevent the upwelling of sadness at regular intervals. Ellen had already warned him that any sustained attack upon him would almost certainly involve images of his loved ones.

For Rosemary, Brook's Corner was a danger zone, and she a dangerous focus for the residents of the house. But her desperate need to help had to be satisfied, and errand girl was the obvious solution.

Bill Suchock just muscled in with the bricklaying, and asked few questions. It was as if he didn't want to know the madness behind the action. He certainly didn't want to hear the talk of 'pathological psychism,' the warning that ill health, or an untreated wound, would attract 'evil' forces. He *knew* that Brook's Corner was a haunted place. He had felt it, after all, and claimed that he could still feel that unnerving presence, even though Brady had most effectively exorcised the rooms!

So Bill kept his mind closed, his back in labour, and worked as hard as the rest, building Brady's wall. It was a good, defensive way to be. A mind occupied with mundanities, and a body in the full sweat of effort, were hard vehicles for psychic possession.

When the attack was heralded, Brady and Ellen were crouched at the Line of Reflection (Ellen's second zone) creating the *zona magnetica*. This began four yards from the Talisman Wall, and followed a parallel course exactly. The *zona magnetica* was designed to snare any elemental force that might penetrate the defences embedded in both the Talisman Wall and the Line of Reflection.

Ellen was showing Brady how to mold the modelling clay around a highly polished nugget of pure iron, creating what she called "gargoyles."

"Press the clay into shapes, anything that comes to mind. Let your hand do the work of your unconscious mind, but think *consciously* of defensive power being impressed into the gargoyle. The iron acts as a receiver; the clay is earth, and when we bury the shape in the ground we are burying a symbol of our unconscious *wish* for defence."

Brady manipulated and kneaded the sticky clay; he made vaguely animal shapes, pressing the distorted features into the soft matrix. The shapes were weird, almost grotesque. They buried them alternately, one of Brady's then one of Ellen's, at five yard intervals along the edge of the *zona magnetica*.

It was as they buried the sixth gargoyle that Ellen looked up sharply, slightly alarmed.

"What can you hear?" she asked Brady quietly. There was a man close by, mixing cement for the wall, and she didn't want her voice to carry.

Brady leaned back on his haunches, staring across the garden and listening. After a moment he heard a distant tinkling sound, like bells. He looked round, but could see nothing. It

was early evening of a very overcast day, and the light was
growing extremely poor.

He queried the sound with Ellen. She rose to her feet and
beckoned him to do the same. She was staring around her,
hard and concerned. To the man working nearby she said,
"Can you hear something, like bells?"

"Bells?" The man stopped working, straightened and listened hard. After a second he shrugged and shook his head.
"All I can hear is chatter."

Brady knew why. Only targeted people could hear the
sounds that accompanied the approach of an attacking elemental. The sounds came in various forms, as bells, as thuds
or creaks, sometimes as a distant banshee wailing. There was
no way of telling, from those simple auditory manifestations,
how strong the assault would be.

"Quickly," she said. "It'll come through the weak point."

"Which weak point?"

"Where it can draw upon local earth energy. If we can
observe it, we'll know where to dig . . ."

"Dig for what? Surely not the villa. That's supposed to be
below the woods."

Ellen raised her hand to silence him. They were approaching
the part of the garden which overlooked the dirt trackway.
Brady noticed that the sound of distant bells had receded from
his awareness.

"Not a whole villa," she said quietly. "Part of it. Perhaps
some of the living quarters, or the servants' quarters. I can't
be sure, but there is *definitely* a fragment of psychic recorder
below the soil level. And it's somewhere on this side of the
house."

Bill Suchock was working on the wall behind the high,
weatherproofed fencing that began the separation between the
neighbouring gardens. He had hung his jacket on a protruding
nail, and was bent busily to the task of raising bricks around a
tiny linen talisman that Ellen had implaced in the wall at that
point. He was increasingly distracted by the gloomy light, and
would have to stop work soon.

The fence in front of him was suddenly struck with immense
violence.

The blow had been startlingly loud, almost like a shot, and

Suchock jumped out of his skin. "What the fuck was that?" he said loudly, as he stood up straight and stared at the fence. A moment later the fencing was violently shaken, the wooden slats splitting and cracking, a sound that was exaggeratedly loud in the still evening. The savage assault lasted just seconds and then the fence stopped moving and there was an abrupt silence.

Puzzled and slightly angry, Suchock climbed onto the low wall and peered over into the other garden to see who was causing the damage.

There was no one there at all.

"Get down from the wall!"

He turned in surprise, and with some alarm saw Dan Brady standing there, face pale, arm extended, beckoning him down. "Quickly Bill! Get down!"

"What's going on, Dan? Who hit the fence?" He could see Ellen Bancroft standing behind Brady, her body slightly hunched. She was staring at the wall, head turning slowly as if she were watching someone move around the garden.

Before Brady could say a word, a section of fencing, ten yards away, was explosively shattered, with a screeching and rending sound that was only part natural. Fragments of wood, and a hail of splinters, sprayed across the garden, and Ellen flung her body round, yelling with pain as her exposed flesh was struck. "It's coming through!" she screamed, and turned back to the breach in the fence.

Bill Suchock turned and fled, ignorant of what was going on, just aware that he wanted no part of it.

Where the fence had been broken, the wall was now attacked and crushed, whole bricks and brick-shards being flung up into the air and across the lawns. A half-brick struck one of the workmen as he gaped at the storm of fury at the bottom of the garden, the blow sending him reeling, blood pouring from gashed flesh. Through the gap in the wall an icy wind blew, accompanied by an eerie wailing sound. Dirt, dust and cement whirled into the dusk sky before this wind, a stinging vortex that blurred the vision.

Ellen had run to the breach, and Brady followed. "It's not as strong as a Stalker," she shouted against the howling gale. "Try the pentagram . . ."

Brady made the air sign towards the invisible energy source, and felt his hand taken and twisted, his arm yanked in an effort to stop him making the symbol. He took a step forward, closer to the wall. He felt hands on his throat, and an intense pressure on his abdomen, a stifling presence around him threatening to suffocate him. Blind fury surfaced in his mind and body: an image of the darkness, and the pain of his near murder. He retaliated in kind, reaching out to strike the elemental, filling his mind with the idea of its destruction.

And quite suddenly there was silence. The wind dropped with impossible abruptness. The noise died away. The oppressive presence vanished from around Brady, and Ellen straightened up, breathing deeply, clearly relieved. She showed Brady her palms, soaked with blood from where she had unwittingly dug her nails into the flesh. She had five small puncture wounds on her face, and she dabbed at them with her handkerchief.

"We beat it off," Brady said. "It went away." The attack had lasted no more than a minute.

"It was tentative," she replied. "There was very little of the mind of the man in it. It was more than a Watcher, but still very tenuous. Such attacks can usually be countered by a strong belief in their destruction."

"What about all the violence?"

"Shedding of psychic energy. It didn't expect to find defences. It tried to get through, expending energy as it failed, and withdrew." She glanced towards the site of its first breaching. "There."

Brady looked across the garden. Three workmen had returned and were talking heatedly among themselves as they stared at the broken fencing. The man who had been hurt was up at the house, having his cut tended to.

There would be some awkward explanations to make, Brady knew. But for the moment he said, "What's there?"

"Dig and find out," said Ellen. "A source of earth energy that attracted the Watcher. It still couldn't penetrate the first line defence, not effectively. But it will . . ."

As they reached the area, Brady said, "It could have attacked in full strength and defeated us."

"It's not an *it*, it's a *man*. And the man is tired, and he's gathering his resources. That was part Watcher, part force that he caused to visit us. It knows about our first line, now, and almost certainly about the *zona magnetica*. As he reabsorbs his thought-form, so *he* will know about them. I think he'll attack with real fury next. It'll be his only chance . . ."

They stared at the ground below them. Ellen said, "Okay, we have to convert this area into a power for *us*. Where's Bill? I want an excavation over twenty feet square to see what lies below."

But Bill Suchock had fled, taking his car and driving home without further thought. When Brady spoke to him on the phone, later, he was shaken, angry and quite adamant that he would not return to help. "I don't know what the fuck you're into, Dan, but man you can count me out. That was no kid doing that. You've got hell itself against you, and I'm not ready to be taken just yet. I must have been mad to have come in the first place."

There was little point in trying to persuade Bill any other way. Not just yet. And then again, maybe it was unreasonable to expose another member of his family to danger.

Brady realized that it was selfishness which motivated his need for Bill Suchock; he liked having the man around. Suchock was solid, firm, clear-thinking; a pragmatic man who brought a certain realism to Brady's increasingly unreal life.

The labourers stood around, disturbed and confused, for an hour. Brady and Ellen told them nothing, merely emphasized the urgency of building the wall higher. Two of the men were set to the task of digging down into the ground where Ellen believed there to be some fragment of an ancient building. The others returned to the wall, but worked in twos, now, and a little more hastily.

By noon of the following day Brady and Ellen were standing at the edge of a pit, three feet deep, which had exposed a shattered, much disturbed mosaic floor. By using a degree of imagination Brady could make out the vague outline of a human figure, and an animal shape next to it. The predominant colour of the Roman flooring was blue. A great deal of mosaic had been dug up by the inexperienced excavators.

"Fantastic," said Brady, bending to touch the cold marble surface.

Ellen was delighted. "I expected a hypocaust, with a skull, or bones, someone killed and buried below the flooring. But this . . ." Abruptly she became business-like, turning to the workmen: "I want two hundred of the central tiles taken up and wrapped in little linen bags." The workmen looked astonished. Ellen ignored them, and said to Brady, "You've got some linen sheets, haven't you? Somewhere? I have no linen left."

"Probably."

"It'll have to be evenly smeared with our blood, then cut into squares. Each tile wrapped in the bag will turn its influence in our favour. Place the tiles along the four foot level of the wall, spread evenly. Is that clear?"

Dumb silence from the perplexed workmen. Again Ellen ignored them, cradling two of the mosaics in her sore hand. She shook her head. "It's just what you said, Dan. Fantastic. Even I can feel the power in them. Whatever happened on that floor, it involved death. The mosaic has imprisoned an astonishing amount of energy."

"How can you *feel* that?"

She passed him the tiles. They sat in his warm hand, cold and hard. He felt strangely calm. He seemed to grow, to become strong. The blue tiles vibrated, grew warm, sent a tingling charge into his skin.

"Imagination," he said, and smiled. Ellen reached out and patted his face affectionately, but indicating: you know better by now.

Two days later the Talisman Wall had reached a height of nearly five feet, and the bricks were finished. Suchock had badly miscalculated, or perhaps he had thought the rubble from the old wall would contain more usable brick than in fact it had. Brady called his brother-in-law, after debating within himself whether he really *wanted* the wall any higher, and managed to get Suchock's promise of a further delivery.

The seven labourers went home, each clutching a substantial cash payment for their efforts. Brady walked about the wall, observing the marks which indicated the various embedded talismans and power-foci, and the line of soot-blackened metal squares attached to the brick at a height of one yard.

They had now built the first three zones of defence, and Ellen was at work marking out the fourth. This ran between ten and fifteen yards from the line of buried clay and iron, and was something of a mystery to Brady. Ellen had prepared an alchemist's nightmare of crushed herbs, splinters of various woods, powdered elements and incense. Brady was made to beat out small sheets of industrial bronze—purloined by Ellen from the Ennean Institute—into shallow dishes. These were placed at intervals along the line of what Ellen called the *zona mandragora*. Mandragora was her name for mandrake, which she had gathered some months before, and which was an essential ingredient of the more powerful defence layer.

"In the middle ages," she had said to Brady, as he watched her preparing the herbal mix, "mandrake was believed to scream when it was pulled from the ground, and that scream could kill. It grew wherever ejaculate fell to the earth, and that most commonly happened below the body of a hanged man. The old alchemists believed it was essential to slit the ground in a circle around the mandrake with an iron sword, then tie the plant to a black dog. Throw meat to the dog and as it ran it would yank the mandrake from the earth." She smiled. "The dog would die from the plant's screams, but the potency of the plant was still immensely high."

"What a lot of nonsense."

"Yes."

"How did you gather it?"

Ellen looked slightly uncomfortable. "Mandrake can't kill, of course. The mediaeval ritual was superstition more than anything. Almost certainly."

"*Almost* certainly?" Brady leaned closer. Ellen busied herself with the pestle and mortar. The smell of the pounded herbs couldn't mask the subtle body perfume of the woman, who, since moving to Brook's Corner, had begun to make an effort towards her personal appearance. Her hair was trimmed (the cuttings burnt), her nails likewise, and she had bought new clothes. Brady said, "How *did* you gather the mandrake? You just pulled it up, of course."

"I didn't think there was any point in taking unnecessary risks," the woman said, flushing slightly. She looked up at Brady, who was staring at her and shaking his head slowly.

She smiled sweetly. "But the black dog didn't die. I swear it."

The importance of mandrake, Ellen had explained, was that it contained an organic chemical which could effectively block psychic transmission. She knew this from elementary work at the Ennean Institute, which had studied various mediaeval 'black' herbs, and discovered these potent chemical blockages to telepathic and extrasensory transmission. Others had the opposite effect, helbane, for instance. But the *zona mandragora* was an extremely effective psychic wall.

"And how many of these zones are we going to need altogether?" Brady had asked.

"Five, if I've got my research right. We also need an Earth Maze zone—a *mazon*. That's easy enough, but God, it's effective. We need to cut the turf into the patterns. I'll show you. Each maze must be connected. The effect is that any elemental or psychic substance that gets that far will become trapped in the maze, and eventually absorbed by the earth. I'm going to scatter trap-sites through all the zones. I'll need mirrors, mercury, sulphur and something with a very precise crystal lattice. Commercial salt is not good enough. Diamond we wouldn't get in sufficient bulk. Quartz would be ideal, because it's almost as hard as diamond and would be hard to break."

Brady had listened to all this, then shaken his head. It seemed like madness, like childish horror movie stuff. And yet here he was, days later, hands dirty from fashioning clay gargoyles and burying them in the ground, fingers blistered from smearing his own bodily exudates on a brick wall, back aching from brick laying and digging; and the cold presence on his chest of a Roman marble tile, scratched with his personal seal —devised by Ellen—and a secret name in which he had encompassed *himself*, and which had thus become him. That name was covered with candle wax, so that it could not be seen. He would wear it as a talisman, but if his attacker came to know the symbolic name that was Daniel Brady, then Brady would weaken against the attack. Whilst the name was secret, and attached to the ancient focus of residual earth energy—the mosaic tile—he was strongly defended against any but the most resolute and brilliant of psychic assassins.

Outside the front of the house he heard a car's horn repeatedly sounded; it was almost angry. Ellen looked up sharply from where she was driving a small hole into the turf of the back lawn. "Who the hell could that be?"

"I don't know. I'll go and look." Brady strolled round the house and along the drive.

Parked across the road from the front gates was Rosemary Suchock's car; Rosemary herself leaned against the driver's door, the window down, her hand resting on the horn.

"About time!" she said sourly as Brady appeared at the gate.

Brady was puzzled. "Rosie . . . what the hell's going on? Why don't you come in?"

Rosemary's pallid features distorted into a grimace as she shook her head. "In there? You must be mad. I'm not stepping inside the gates." She was more angry than Brady had ever seen her; she was practically shaking with outrage. "I don't know what you've got in there, or what you've done, but you're not going to destroy *me; or* Bill. That's what I've come to say to you, Dan. Leave Bill alone, I mean it!"

Brady crossed the road to her, but when he reached out his hand to take her arm she twisted away. "Don't touch me!"

"Rosie! For Christ's sake!"

"Don't touch me!" she shouted. "I mean it, Dan! Leave us alone. Leave Bill alone!" She had crossed her arms over her chest, and stood defiantly before him, the anger making her face into something ugly, almost feral. "I'm not going to have my family destroyed like yours was. I'm not having Bill go the way of Alison. Bill's intending to come here again, even though I begged him not to. If anything happens to him, Dan, so help me God, I'll kill you! I'll fucking well kill you!"

She's right, he thought. She's right. I must be out of my mind to involve Bill in this. It's so unfair. I have no right to risk Bill's life.

Rosie may not have known what was going on, but she had intuited the danger, and that sense of growing danger was slowly driving her crazy . . .

"I'm sorry, Rosie—"

"Never mind sorry! Just leave us alone, Dan. Let us alone. I want to live my life with my husband and my child, without haunting, without the feeling of being watched, without having Bill wake up screaming at night, and talking about fences being blasted by unseen people, and bricks thrown across gardens. *We have the right to our own lives! You're destroying us!"*

Her voice had risen to an hysterical screech, her face red with fury, tears squeezing from her eyes. She started to sob, and to shake violently, and Dan wrapped his arms around her, and although she struggled for a moment she finally let her resistance go, and wept against his chest.

"Okay Rosie, I get the message. When Bill comes along here later I'll not let him go through the gates. I'll leave you alone until this mess is sorted out."

As if she had suddenly sensed something appalling about Brady, Rosemary jerked away from him, wrapped her arms around herself and stood trembling, staring up at her brother. "I'm going out of my mind, Dan. With worry, with fear . . . I'm sorry for you. I truly am. For Alison . . . you know how I feel . . . but you're a dead man. I don't know what happened to you, what part of you was destroyed by grief, or the beating you received, or what. But you're dead to me, Dan. Bill thought you were dead when he found you. But I know it for a fact. You're cold. Ice cold. If we stay around you, we'll be cold too. I'm not having that . . ."

"I understand, Rosie. Go home. We'll talk on the phone—"

She almost screamed the word, almost burst a blood vessel with the power and energy of what she screeched at him: *"Nothing! Nothing! Leave! Us! ALONE!"*

And she pushed roughly past him and into her car, which skidded away down the road, swaying dangerously before it straightened up and vanished into the distance.

— FOURTEEN

THAT EVENING, Andrew Haddingham visited the house, bringing two boxes of much needed food supplies, his shotgun, and a box half full of cartridges. Brady was grateful for the loan of the gun. His brother-in-law, too, had promised to obtain a shotgun for him. The extra defence might have been impractically physical, but was nevertheless reassuring.

Haddingham stayed to eat. While he was there he inspected, and was duly impressed and confused by, the psychic defences around Brook's Corner. Ellen explained them as Brady cooked the light supper. While they ate there was a strained silence, and afterwards, digesting their meal in cosy silence, Brady sensed a tension in the air, a vague form of discomfort. He thought he detected it in Ellen too, a restlessness that made the meeting with Haddingham less pleasurable than it should have been. Brady couldn't understand it, and at first assumed that they were being targeted. Something inside him told him that that was not the case.

Haddingham, too, could feel the unease, and with his usual gracious charm he excused himself, at about seven-thirty, and made his way home. Brady and Ellen then tackled the nightly routine of changing the beds around.

Ellen had already explained in detail the need to avoid routine; Brady regularly changed his clothes, bathed, and never sat in the same chair too long. Each night, with Ellen's help, he changed the position of his bed through ninety degrees.

Tonight he would change rooms, stripping the beds totally for the wash, he taking Dominick's room where Ellen had been sleeping, and she taking Marianna's. By this regularly altered routine there could be no build-up of static energy from their individual auras, a magnetism that could attract psychic substance from outside and which would help the focussing of any attacking mind.

It was as they stripped the sheets in the main bedroom that their fingers touched, just briefly, and although they were well used to physical contact in moments of danger or great tension, this touch was different. Brady felt as if an electric shock had been pulsed through his body. He almost jerked his hand back from the tentative contact, and glanced at Ellen. Her eyes were lowered, her face clearly blushing. A second later she looked up and met his gaze, and Brady was instantly aware of what had been passing between them earlier in the evening.

It had perhaps been creeping up on them for a day or two, a growing awareness of each other, not as two threatened individuals, building a defence together, but as attractive and mutually attracted opposites.

Brady laughed nervously. "I wondered if this would happen."

"If what would happen?"

"That I'd start to want you."

Ellen gathered the crumpled undersheet into her arms, pressing it into a compact ball. She stood there, almost protecting herself from Brady, but looking at him with a soft intensity. "You're thinking of Alison."

Brady wasn't sure whether that was true or not. Certainly, in the last few moments, he had been half aware of the last sexual encounter with Alison, but Ellen was implying that he was concerned with a sense of betrayal, and that wasn't true.

"Not really. Are you thinking of Michael?"

Ellen laughed softly, an almost tired affirmation. "I think of Michael all the time. But I have no considerations about letting him down. To start worrying about betrayal, now, would be a ridiculous form of self-denial. I may be a crazy lady, Dan, but I have an ordinary woman's needs, and I *have* started to want you."

Brady took the bundled sheet from her, and placed it on the

bed. He had intended to reach out for Ellen and kiss her, but in the event they ended hugging each other closely, patting each other on the back, more as if they were reassuring each other than making a pass. "Is it loneliness doing this?" Brady said.

"Don't question things so much. Loneliness perhaps; frustration perhaps. But desire as well." She leaned back, still holding him, and stared up at him, smiling. "I desire you, Dan. I feel it very strongly."

"Me too," he said helplessly, conscious of the inadequacy of that childishly nervous assertion. "You've been smelling good these last couple of days." When Ellen laughed, saying, "What *are* you implying?" Brady laughed too, holding the woman closer to him.

"I didn't mean it that way, I meant . . . I'm becoming conscious of you . . ."

"I knew what you meant," she said softly, and reached up a little so that he could kiss her gently on the lips. The kiss was tentative to begin with, then exploratory, lips parting, tongues touching with more and more determination. Brady felt at once aroused, yet unable to respond. He became embarrassed when his body failed to take note of his desire and his hot, awkward flush interfered with the intimacy of the moment. He disengaged, stepped back, and smiled. "We'd better finish making up the beds."

"Bed," she corrected. "Just one from now on."

They opted to remain in the main room, turned the double-bed through ninety degrees and made it up with crisp, fresh sheets. The silence that hung between them was excited and anticipatory. Brady worried about his socks, which he hadn't changed since working in his garden shoes that morning; Ellen continually glanced at herself in the bedroom mirror, and made fleeting passes at her hair, pulling it back from her face as if she were concerned not to look too unkempt.

She needn't have worried. Brady, having relinquished that defensiveness of mind that had prevented him from assessing Ellen Bancroft fully as a woman, found the American quite gorgeous, her tanned skin and dark features making her at once sultry and erotic. Her hands were small and delicate, and the touch of her fingers had already sent various shivers and tingles through his body; he anticipated her more arousing touch with impatience.

He voiced the only doubt he had held in reserve. "Are you sure that . . . well, that to have sex together won't weaken us? It will take our attention away from more dangerous issues."

"*More* dangerous?" Ellen looked mischievous. "You mean, sex with me is dangerous, but not as dangerous as psychic attack?"

"You know what I mean!"

"Yes. I know what you mean. Don't worry, Dan. It's quite the opposite. Sex will strengthen us, because it will strengthen our individual auras. The act of love, emotionally committed and physically enthusiastic, may tire the muscles, but it strengthens the body incredibly. One literally basks in an afterglow of sex, you've heard that clichéd expression. Two people who make love vigorously strengthen their aura for up to seven or eight hours. It induces confidence, inner well-being. You must have experienced that sensation."

Brady was slightly alarmed. "You're being very clinical."

"I don't mean to be. I'm sorry," she looked genuinely upset, frowning as she said, "I meant what I said about desire, about fancying you. I really do, Dan. But I don't think we can —or should—do anything without understanding the consequences."

"You're quite right. I'm just nervous, Ellen, that's all. I'm not one of your gay philanderers—that's the English 'gay.' I'm not used to starting new relationships. It took me six months to turn an affair with one of my lab assistants from the 'hand-holding, eye-gazing, talking-about-it' stage to the first sexual encounter."

"English isn't the word for it!" said Ellen, with mock horror. "That's positively Victorian!" Brady smiled. Ellen went on, "Don't worry, Dan. It's a useful byproduct of sex that we will strengthen our auras. I'm not going to suggest that we couple each time someone attacks us psychically. Oh God, can you imagine?" Brady could, and he laughed as she laughed. "Humping away furiously, elementals gathered in a big circle, struggling to get in. Uh uh!" She walked back to Brady and took his hands in hers, leaned up and kissed his lips. Her breath was warm and sweet. "I need this, and I need you. I want you very much."

Brady turned on the bedside lamp, then undressed quickly. He found time to dart to the bathroom and wash both his feet in cold water, just to be on the safe side. As he padded quickly back to the bedroom Ellen passed him, on her way to the loo. She still wore her underclothes and Brady glanced back at her, liking her body very much, its slimness, the muscles looking strong in her legs, her breasts fuller than he had thought. He became conscious of his stocky waist, his belly not exactly trim and flat. But he darted under the sheets and waited for her. When she came back to the room she was naked, and smelled faintly of sex. She climbed beneath the sheets and they cuddled for a moment, chilled by the cold bathroom. Brady's fingers found the small scar on her back, and the mole on her left hip. Her fingers prodded his stomach, and gently stroked his nipples.

It was fun, he thought, those first few minutes of exploring a new body. "I think I'm nervous," he said with slight embarrassment. "I'm not tumescent."

"You're not *what*?" she said, with a smirk. "God, you English! And you call *me* 'clinical'. " Her hand moved down his stomach and her finger gently wrapped around his flaccid penis. At once he started to arouse, but his distracted thoughts, and the tension he felt at this first encounter, effectively blocked him from a total rigidity. Her fingers played expertly with him as they kissed more deeply, and he stroked and pressed her hard-tipped breasts.

"I'm not going to make it," he said as he pulled away from her. Her hand remained on him as he frowned. "Sorry," he said, and was startled as she said the word "sorry" in total unison with him. She chuckled. "I knew you were going to say it. Michael always . . . oh, sorry!" she broke off quickly, realizing how inappropriate she had been about to be. Brady laughed and prodded her chest with his forefinger. "You Americans!" he teased.

"Lie back."

He did as he had been bidden and Ellen's head disappeared beneath the sheets. Her mouth on him was warm and firm, her teeth a gently nipping sensation, and after a moment he threw back the sheets and held her head, moving her up and down along his member, thrilled at the sight of what she was doing. He was ready for her in seconds, and when she straightened up again, and reached her arms around his neck, he moved on top of her, guided by her. She requested, and required no foreplay from him. She was moistly ready for him and they took each other vigorously and noisily for nearly ten minutes before they came in unison and lay still again, fingers entwined, heads touching, but faces turned away from each other.

Brady woke abruptly at 3:13 in the morning. He had been violently dreaming, and in the dream had been running through the streets, the sound of his footfall a regular and echoing *thud*. As he came awake, and alert, so that thudding sound persisted for a few seconds before dying away.

Ellen was sitting bolt upright beside him. In the dimness Brady could see that her eyes were wide with shock. "Did you hear something?" he said.

"That sound," she said. "Like thudding footsteps. That's it, like the ringing bells."

"The Stalker."

"Quick," she said, swinging her legs out of the bed. "We've got to light the braziers." She struggled into her towelling robe, but Brady didn't bother with clothing. He ran naked down the stairs and to the back door of the house. The cold air hit him hard, but he ignored it, running into the garden with the lighter he had bought for just this purpose. He went along the line setting the powdered herbs smouldering, and in two or three minutes had managed to light every brazier. The clear air became tainted with the acrid odour of the incense. Against the half moon, Brady could see the trickles of dark smoke rising into the night.

"Put something on!" Ellen called from the back door. She stood there, huddled in her robe, staring into the darkness.

"I'm not cold," Brady called back. It was a lie, and yet it wasn't. His skin was cold, yes, but he himself felt hot, angry. He prowled around the edge of the *mazon*, close to the house, his eyes keen for the slightest movement. "Where are you?" he muttered loudly, and then raised his voice to shout.

"Where are you, dammit? Show yourself!"

"Dan! Don't be a fool." Ellen's voice was not persuasive enough.

"I'm going to face it, Ellen. I want it to know who it's up against."

He heard movement at the bottom of the garden, and ran lithely and lightly towards it, staying within the *zona mandragora*. As he followed the sound he knew that his words of a moment ago had been irrational and arrogant. Yes, something within him was determined not to be subdued, or scared, by the psychic creature that was being projected against him. He knew, perhaps by instinct, that he had to start to face the attacker.

"Shout at the devil," he said to himself, repeating a cliché he had read or learned as a child.

Beyond the Talisman Wall, something glowed.

It was an area of brightness that dissipated as fast as it formed. It moved along the rough track, and vanished behind the trees. In the half light of the moon, these trees were eerie outlines against the broken cloud.

It struck from the east, with a great wailing shriek and an explosion of wood and brick that showered Brady with splinters of stone and bark and made him cover his eyes. He felt blood on his skin where the jagged fragments of brick had lacerated his flesh. Above the awful howling of the elemental, he could hear Ellen's furious, frantic screaming for him to return to the house.

But Brady, acting on an impulse drawn more from foolhardiness than courage, stood his ground. Before him, the oak where Willie Crinkleleaf had his home was twisted and thrashed by unseen forces. Its upper branches waved madly; its bark split with an agonized groaning sound, but the great tree remained upright. Brick fragments blew at him, and the ground below his feet vibrated and seemed almost to ripple.

Two glowing balls of light appeared on the garden side of the wall and literally flew in opposite directions, hugging the mirrored brick, and at times bobbing up and down and darting towards him, as if trying to break through the unseen barrier of iron and clay. The balls of light coalesced again and formed a burning cross, that began to turn, and became a gi-

gantic catherine wheel. Light, like plasma, flew in all directions. Some of it appeared to land on Brady's skin, but it
neither burned nor persisted. The spinning wheel of flame
changed again, this time into a writhing man-like shape,
features indistinct, its visual qualities fading until it was
merely a half-glimpsed night-shadow, moving rapidly along-
side the wall. Brady raced in pursuit.

The stench of the burning herbs was pungent and irritating.
Brady knocked over one of the smoking braziers. He stumbled, grabbed for it, but failed to prevent it spilling its smouldering contents.

The elemental moved towards him there. The wind that
struck him forcibly in the face was cold and stank like a rotting corpse, making him gag. He stood his ground, pale
bodied, goose-pimpled, nude against the naked power of his
assailant's mind.

"Who are you?" he screamed, searching the writhing
smoke-like form for some sign of a face, some hint of the evil
behind the psychic substance.

"WHO ARE YOU? SHOW YOURSELF."

And with a great shriek, like a carrion bird, the Stalker
came at him, through the magnetic zone of iron and clay,
towering above him, reaching hands towards him. He was
struck on the face by a shard of brick flung by the wind. He
staggered backwards, fetching up hard and cold against the
wall of the house. The garden before him seemed empty, but
the brazier that had fallen was buckled and twisted and finally
flung aside. He watched as the turf within the *zona magnetica*
was ravaged, earth and grass scattered about, and one of
the clay gargoyles finally uprooted and crushed to powder in
mid-air. "Who are you?" shrieked Brady, and stepped back
towards it, tripping on the cut edge of turf where he had fash-
ioned one of the complex mazes.

The wind blew all around him. The moon went in behind a
bank of dark cloud, and there was a sudden, startling silence.
The wind dropped away and the garden was still. Brady
stepped out of the lee of the house and into the *zona mandragora*, walking towards the wall. Beneath his feet the
ground was cold and littered with jagged fragments of brick

which hurt him badly as he stepped upon them.

When he reached the wall he began to slap his hand, palm upwards, against the painted surface. Harder and harder he struck the wall, his mouth drawn back in a grimace of anger and frustration, the tears squeezing from his eyes as he repeated over and over, in rhythm with his steady, painful striking, "Who. *Are*. You? Who. *Are*. You?"

Ellen sat on the edge of the bed and stared at the dishevelled, bleeding man before her. Brady was still shaking. His face was white, save where it was smeared with blood and several dark streaks of grime. He had at least twenty cuts on his body, one of them, on his stomach, bleeding very badly. The blood had drenched his dark pubic hair.

"That was very foolish," she said. "You could have been killed."

"I thought that if I challenged it directly I might sense the mind behind it."

"But you didn't."

He shook his head, walked to the bedroom chair, and sat down, rested his head in his hands and took several deep breaths. "I was frightened," he whispered. "I kept hearing Marianna's voice, almost lost against the wind. But it was her voice."

"It was the voice of the thought-form."

Angrily, Brady said, "I *know* that. You already warned me of it! But it was still . . . it was still *powerful*. It frightened me to hear her voice." Dejectedly he stared at the floor. Softly: "I keep wondering if she's dead. I keep imagining her, buried in woodland somewhere, rats and foxes trying to fight over her . . ." he shivered violently, then again breathed deeply. "I'm a mess," he said, and stood, walking quickly to the bathroom to attend to his cuts and grazes.

Ellen got back into bed. She had watched Brady's senseless confrontation from Marianna's room. What had concerned her most was the strength of the attack. Its radiant energy had affected her despite the depth of zonal defence between her and the elemental. And it had broken the *zona magnetica*! It was using the man's mind far more, then. It might take a day or two to recoup his energy, but he was getting deeper. He was able to come that much closer. Next time he might get to the house itself . . .

They *had* to find out who was projecting the Stalker. They *had* to destroy him, before his hideous creation destroyed them.

Again she felt the revulsion of those hands upon her body. And again she felt the sense of familiarity in the attack, the mind behind the beast aware of her, conscious of her, more involved with her than just a random striker. The names of those she knew flashed through her head again. Names, faces, men she knew, men she had worked with . . . and one man in particular, one man whom she instinctively feared, disliked almost tangibly. But she couldn't base any charge at all on just a whim, just a seventh sense.

She had to know for sure! She had to *see* him.

It made her sick to think about it. But when Brady limped back into the room and climbed unsteadily into the bed, reeking of germoline and iodine, she knew that, all things considered, she had no choice.

Whether she liked it or not she needed Brady. And that meant alive. She couldn't let him risk another fatuous confrontation with something as powerful as this elemental. It would get him nowhere but in his grave.

For all their sakes, and for the sake of Michael and Justin, and all of Brady's family too, she had to tempt the Stalker out again . . .

Attract it to her, and let it attack . . .

—FIFTEEN—

SHE COULD THINK of many things that might have got in the way of her journey home to Islington, but she never expected the encounter in Upper Street.

She had left Brook's Corner at midday, after helping Brady to rebuild the breached defences, and compounding a fresh mix of the mandragora incense. Brady had been subdued, still shaken by his early morning encounter, reacting now, to the shock and the fear that he had repressed during his challenge. And he ached, and was sore, and grumped about his physical discomfort, the more so for hearing Ellen's unsympathetic criticism.

As she left, she had said, "Watch television, read pulp novels, anything to fill your mind with the mundane. Okay? Hot baths if you feel you're being targeted. Eat well. Don't drink. Don't masturbate . . ." she kissed him on the nose and grinned.

"Fill my mind with the mundane?" he queried.

"Sure. It's hard to influence a mind absorbed by Tom and Jerry. There are a hundred little things you can do to maintain your integrity, Dan. You'll learn them all soon. Get Andrew round, or Bill—"

"Bill won't come. And it's too risky."

"Andrew, then. He knows what's going on. Company helps. Fill the house, fill it with talkative mundanes. Just lay off the booze; and no drugs, no solitary walks, and no girls

155

—that's not part of the defence, that's just because I don't want you to."

She had taken a taxi to the station, and arrived shortly after at Paddington. The journey had been uneventful, almost relaxing. It was not until she reached Baker Street, travelling on the underground, that the first prickling sensation of unease struck her. The tube was crowded. She had entered the smokers' compartment by mistake. Two or three of the silent passengers looked up at her audible gasp of shock as she realized she was being targeted, and stared at her. She knew she had gone pale, and that she was radiating the beginnings of fear. But there was nothing she could do about it.

At Kings Cross she left the tube, climbed to the station forecourt and caught a bus to Islington.

The Watcher pursued her. She was unsure whether or not it was purely a Watcher, or the more sinister, and destructive form of elemental that had been sent against Brook's Corner. From this distance it was very hard to tell. What appalled her was that the presence pursued so easily. It was no paranoid fantasy of hers. When she looked round, when she studied the crowds, she could observe the unconscious movement of the masses around, and away from, a focus of energy that they couldn't appreciate with their senses, but were nevertheless responding to.

Unless the man behind it were following her himself, this thought-form was stretched to a very long range. It had come against her in her apartment several times, but she had always assumed that its source was close by. Now she was not so sure.

This man was more powerful than she had imagined. A true adept. A true long range.

She left the bus just before Upper Street and strode briskly towards the small park at the bottom of Essex Road, picking up two or three items from the chemist on the way.

And it was then that she heard a familiar voice: "Ellen! Ellen Bancroft!"

Good God, she thought with horror. David Marchant! Oh Christ. What the hell is *he* doing here?

Never in all her wildest bad dreams could she have envisioned something so inconvenient at this moment as a chance encounter with an ex-lover, and a man with whom she had

worked at the Ennean. She glanced round, praying that she
was mistaken, but no; there he was, chasing after her.

David Marchant. God forbid.

She tried to ignore him, increasing her pace, but he puffed
and panted after her, and finally she could not bring herself to
keep walking. She had no antipathy towards Marchant at all.
She just didn't want to be bothered with him, now. She knew
that he had been desperately anxious at her disappearance,
several months ago, but according to Andrew Haddingham he
had made little effort to trace her, after the first few days of
confusion in her department. So she decided to be cold,
abrupt, and spare him the risk of danger. "What do you want,
David?"

"Ellen," he said. He was confused and gasping for breath,
and she could see by his eyes that he was disappointed at her
coolness. "Ellen, where on earth have you been?"

"What do you *want*, David?"

"Just to talk, Ellen. It's been six months or more . . .
What's happened to you? You look ill . . ."

He had always been the clinging sort. During their affair he
had become complacent, dependent, glad to go along with her
every whim, unwilling to assert himself. He responded best—
and most positively from Ellen's point of view—to cold anger.

She said, "Fuck off, David!" then turned on her heel and
paced away. Real anger grew in her. He was such a weak man.
He knew what had happened to her family; he must have been
aware that she was a focus of danger. Haddingham had said
that *some* understanding of her tragedy had filtered through
to her old friends. Marchant persisted. Again she shouted at
him, "Go away, David. I beg you, for *your* sake, for *my* sake,
just *leave me alone*."

The interchange of words continued. Ellen dragged herself
away, but he followed.

And suddenly it was there, no more than forty yards distant. Its presence was tangible, horrifying, close. She could
smell it, she could almost hear its breathing. She was a quarter
of a mile from her safe apartment, and Marchant was slowing
her down.

Awful panic surged through her breast. Thoughts tumbled
through her head: it had attached itself to Marchant; Mar-

chant was the man behind the elemental; Marchant was being used, a carrier, strengthening the elemental which was so distant from its source. Paranoid confusion raged. She screamed at the gaping man before her. "You! It's with you! You've led it here!"

Even as she said the words, turning to run at the same time, she knew that she was just rationalizing what she would have to do next.

She would never make the apartment. It would catch her first, and if it was more than a Watcher . . .

When David Marchant's hand grasped her arm, she reached quickly into her bag and uncorked the small vial she kept there. She dipped her nails into the pungent cream, a mix of her own blood, urine and skin tissue, then slashed out quickly at Marchant's face, drawing blood.

Thus she marked him. He carried the scent of her, potently on his skin, and it would attract the Watcher for a moment or two, and give her the chance to make it home.

I'm sorry, David, she thought as she ran. I'm so sorry. If only you hadn't turned up.

She made the safety of her apartment in a minute or two and watched from the window as the bemused figure of David Marchant entered the garage court and stood there, looking about him. He was touching his cheek tenderly. He couldn't understand either the reason, or the nature, of that uncalled-for attack.

Marked as he was, he sensed the Stalker as it came through the alley way and into the courtyard. Ellen tried to close her ears to his shrill and terrible scream; but she felt forced to watch as his body was crushed and twisted, then flung from the fire-escape onto the concrete roadway.

She kept the lights in her apartment out. She sat on the edge of the bed and watched the flickering blue of the police lamps below, reflected on her darkened window. Three times her doorbell was rung, and she remained silent and still. She heard the police talking to her neighbour, asking about the occupancy of Flat 3. The neighbour knew nothing, but thought that the occupant was away.

The police left it at that.

It was four hours before the ambulance removed Marchant's body; but the police task force remained below in strength, examining every inch of ground. The lights continued to flash; uniformed police, and plain clothes men, swarmed about the area. Several times she heard footsteps on the fire-escape and moved to hide behind the door. She was aware of the faces that peered into her flat, trying the windows. But it was not unlikely that a resident would be away, and the examination of her rooms was cursory.

She thought they would never leave. By eleven the task force below had shrunk to about four men; by cautiously peering out of her windows she could see that uniformed police had been stationed at the front of the block of flats.

The same would no doubt be true of the rear entrance.

At midnight she risked a phone call to Brady, who was still up and wide awake. It was good to hear his voice; almost reassuring. They talked for ten minutes, Brady not pressing her for details of the killing outside her flat, nor for details of what she was feeling. They just talked. Mostly of the night before.

At two in the morning Ellen went about the flat and broke the seals on windows and doors. She sneaked out onto the fire-escape and terminated the defences there. Shaking like a leaf, more vulnerable than she had ever been before, she went back to her bed and sat on the edge.

What the hell am I doing?

She began to cry, stifling the sound, but allowing the tears to flood down her cheeks and drop unchecked onto her skirt. She tried to imagine Michael's arm around her, and Justin's plaintive voice: "It's all right, Mum. Don't cry . . ." She tried to remember the smells of the flat they had shared, and the cold, country freshness of the tiny cottage where she and Michael had first lived, in Sussex. The memories were strong, poignant. She clung to them desperately, they were so vivid. She had not been this close to Michael for months. Her shoulder tingled with his touch, his gentle fingers stroking her, reassuring her . . .

Such a gentle touch . . .

Fingers on her breasts . . .

A touch on her face, her throat. The smell of decay!

She screamed and sat bolt upright, her skin immediately breaking into a sweat. The touch on her body ceased. The room was not quite in total darkness; moonlight cast the shadow of her wardrobe on the far wall. The mirror was a bright reflection on the paintwork.

It was in the room with her!

The terror that instantly possessed Ellen made her gorge rise and her body begin to shake; a single rational thought filled her mind; I can't go through with this. *I can't go through with this!*

On legs that felt as if they would hardly support her, she rushed from the bedroom and into the lounge, switching on the light as she went. The sudden brilliance lasted only for a second before the bulb exploded noisily and the darkness returned.

She backed up against the wall, staring into the room, aware of the presence before her, watching her. "Oh God no!" she said softly, then began to make the pentagram in the air.

Her hand felt as if it were moving through water. The action was slow, restricted. Eventually she couldn't move her arm at all. She began to slip down the wall, sobbing, until she was seated awkwardly on the floor. She felt her arms lifted by powerful hands and held above her head. She began to struggle, tearful, but silent, not allowing the scream that she so desperately wanted to express to emerge.

There was breath on her face, and the force that held her secure began to explore her body, a touch that was as tentative as it was relentless, finding every part of her, moving through her clothes, pinching her flesh painfully, probing, rubbing, pressing . . .

And then the words, whispered to her, whispered *at* her, like the obscene ramblings of an unseen man, on the end of a phone, through a wall, in her darkest dreams . . .

Wantyouwantyouyourbodyloveyousohardalwayswanted youtouchyoumakelovetoyoulieonyournakedbodybreastsin myhandlipstouchingfuckinggentlyellenellenwantyouallthe timelookatmelookatmelookatme

. . . and though the words began as a low, animal growling, the voice changed, became more human, a whispered voice whose tones she began to recognize. The touch on her body became more insistent, more painful. She didn't fight it. She concentrated on the foul stream of suggestion, trying to hear beyond the obscenity to the voice itself, and as she listened, as she encouraged the words to continue, so she began to recognize that voice, and it was as she had suspected. She felt sick, now, to listen to the filthy words and imagine the middle-aged features of George Campbell, the Director of Hillingvale. These were his thoughts, these were the thoughts that had surged and pulsed at the back of his mind all the time she had been in his presence, talking about projects, discussing psychometry and telepathy, working so hard, so enthusiastically, so glad of this important friend in the field. And he had sat there, chewing on his pipe, and talking back to her, and all the time his mind had been filled with these lustful, disgusting thoughts. She felt sick at the idea of it. She had known it, she supposed, she had sensed it, but to be a party to that incoherent jumble of frustrated desire was appalling; sickening.

She wanted to scream abuse, to shout his name and let him know, as loudly as possible, just how contemptuous she felt about him. But she resisted the temptation. She realized that if she let the elemental know what she had discerned, then Campbell himself would soon know, and his tactic might change such that her plan of action, her plan to snare the Stalker, would not be able to go ahead.

She tried to close her mind to everything; she tried to close off her senses to the ghostly assault upon her. She deliberately remembered parts of her training.

Auditory signals of psychic attack: a sound like the ringing of bells, a creaking sound, and rhythmic thudding. Spoken words are suspicious, and more likely to be auditory hallucination...

The words began to fade away...

She could hardly believe it when the touch upon her body vanished as well, leaving her bruised and shaken, tasting the blood on her lips. She stared into the darkened room, breathing heavily, shaking as she anticipated a renewed assault upon her.

What had happened?

She had been convinced that if she allowed the elemental to approach again it would attack her more viciously and completely than before. Perhaps it had withdrawn and was even now watching her from the darkness, waiting to approach again and kill her. But she knew Campbell's unconscious desire for her had tempered the murderous qualities of his creation, and he would have to summon a new elemental if he were to attack her *without* the undertone of sexual intent.

Slowly she pushed herself to her feet, sliding up the wall, eyes wide. Her legs were in pain, and she knew she was bruised. The blood that flooded her mouth was sour and unpleasant, but she swallowed hard, unwilling to leave any traces of her body on the floor of the flat. Slowly she picked her way to the bedroom and turned on the light.

After a few minutes her body ceased to shake. The Stalker had gone. Perhaps it was now moving towards Brook's Corner, and Brady would find himself up against it yet again.

Right now Ellen didn't care. She made herself a cup of strong, black coffee, and sipped it as she phoned for a taxi. It was nearly three a.m. The encounter had lasted the better part of an hour, and yet it seemed no more than a brutal five minutes.

If she could get past the uniformed policeman, stationed outside, she could be at Brook's Corner at dawn.

─ SIXTEEN ──────────

HE WOKE TO the gentle purring of the phone beside his bed. His wife stirred restlessly, but did not wake. He sat up and glanced at the clock: four in the morning. His head buzzed with fatigue, and as he reached for the phone he recognized that particular exhaustion that meant he had been transmitting.

No! It can't be!

"Hello? he said quietly into the phone. And thought, *I've been asleep. I can't have been transmitting. In the name of God, what's happening to me?*

"Wickhurst?"

"Yes. Speaking."

He was drained. He was totally drained. He could feel the knot in his solar plexus where the link reached out to the psychic substance of his own mind. It was drawing close, returning. *In sleep he had been transmitting!*

The man at the other end of the phone spoke slowly and deliberately, the tone almost patronizing. "Are you experiencing difficulty?"

He shivered, with cold perhaps, or with fear. "I don't know."

"Is he killed?"

"No. He's created partial defences around his house. He has the woman with him. Ellen Bancroft."

"Are you experiencing difficulty?"

He knew what it would mean to say yes. *I mustn't admit it.* "His strength was unexpected. I know the measure of him, now."

The voice at the other end of the phone almost hissed as it spoke. "Will he be killed?"

"I understand him now. I can take him."

"And the woman." It was a statement.

"Yes. She too."

"Why is it taking so long? Are you experiencing difficulty?"

"No. No difficulty. He is able to detach his persona, and it is a strong manifestation. I had not expected that. But I understand him now. I will take care of it."

"And the woman?"

"I will take care of them both."

There was a pause on the phone. His wife shifted in bed and made incoherent sounds as her sleep was disturbed.

Then the voice again: "Arachne is returning to the south. They have sent a mandrathon to you . . ."

NO! OH GOD NO! NOT THAT!

"Please . . ." he said, trying to keep the panic from his voice, "it's not necessary. I swear it."

"The mandrathon is coming. I'll ask again. Are you experiencing difficulty?"

What do I say? In heaven's name, what do I say?

"No. No difficulty. I will create the elemental now. How long do I have?"

"You have a few hours. At least until dusk."

"Thank you."

He placed the phone gently back on the receiver, and remained quite still for a few moments, staring at it. Then he reached into his bedside drawer for the two photographs he always kept there. He stared at them and the bitterness and anger within him grew.

Beside him his wife slept on, unaware of the sounds of hatred and frustration that her husband uttered as he slowly and deliberately crushed the photographs in his hand.

"What the hell are you doing up so early?"

Brady looked startled as Ellen entered the dining room of

Brook's Corner, where he was seated, cleaning and inspecting the shotgun that Andrew Haddingham had loaned him. It was just before six in the morning. Outside, the garden was covered with frosted dew, and the dining room itself was cold, the windows patterned with ice.

"I haven't been to bed," Brady replied. He looked tired, he knew, and he felt very weary. But the sight of Ellen Bancroft enlivened him, and he stood to kiss her. Ellen herself looked as if she had been a week without sleep. Her eyes were puffy, her hair dishevelled, and she was frozen. Brady rubbed her hands vigorously. "You look exhausted."

"I am. Totally. I'll grab a little sleep before I begin building."

She stripped off her coat and began to unpack her bag, placing a variety of items and boxes on the table. Brady watched her curiously. It had been a long night for him, crouched in a room, protected by a circle and various primitive defences, dreading the return of the Stalker while he was alone. But he knew that for Ellen the night had been far longer, far more harrowing.

"Was it . . ." he began, meaning to ask if her experiences had been as bad as he imagined. He found the words dried up on his lips. It was such a personal thing that she may have been through that somehow it did not seem right for him to enquire. And yet he was concerned for her, anxious for her well-being . . . and hungry for whatever information she may have gleaned during her ordeal.

"Was it what?" she said wearily, and glanced at him tiredly as she sat down in one of the easy chairs, kicked off her shoes, and stretched out her legs. "Was it rough?" She lay her head back and closed her eyes. Brady watched her. "Yes. It was rough. But it wasn't as bad as I'd expected." She stopped speaking. Brady stared at the objects on the table, idly wondering what she was intending to build. Another trap, no doubt. He had given up trying to comprehend the full extent of Ellen's acquired knowledge.

As if she sensed that he was still sitting there, about to ask more questions, she opened her eyes, regarded him blearily and said. "Listen. I don't want to talk about it. I really don't. It was bad. I want to forget it."

"I can understand that," Brady said quietly.

"The thing you need to know . . ." she regarded him squarely, tired eyes narrowed. "Our man is George Campbell. I had a hint before, but I couldn't be certain. Now I'm sure. The source is George Campbell."

Brady had already jumped to his feet, with shock and surprise, leaning on the table and staring at the American. "Campbell! Are you sure?"

"Quite sure."

"Good God Almighty!" he bellowed. "George Campbell . . . I can't believe it. It can't be true . . ."

"It's true," said Ellen tiredly. She had closed her eyes again. "I need sleep."

Brady stared into the distance, mouth open, letting the full impact of th revelation sink in. Campbell, the highly respected Director of Hillingvale. Campbell! A man with political contacts almost growing out of his body. Rich, arrogant, brilliant, a man destined for the sort of honours and accolades, on his eventual retirement, that only the very, very best in their fields achieve.

"I worked with him," he said softly, angrily. "I've sat in the same room as him, given him ideas, I listened to what he had to say. I've learned to respect him, even if I hated him. He never liked me, but I always felt he admired my work. Campbell! The bastard . . . one of them, one of the attackers. He always liked Alison. He used to make her feel uncomfortable with his overweening attention, at socials, when he invited us to dinner once. I never guessed . . . it never occurred to me . . ." he squeezed his eyes shut, feeling tears of anger and grief bubbling for expression. "*Campbell!*" he repeated, the tension in his body making him express the name through clenched teeth. When he looked at Ellen she was staring at him blankly, letting him ride the shock, and the fear, and the anger . . .

"He was the same with me," she said. "Perhaps worse. I was naïve enough to be flattered by his attention, by his warmth. I saw prospects, promotion, a brilliant reference from a man of amazing stature. I was unlikely to get a good reference from my own supervisor, Geoffrey Dean. I think Campbell wanted me from the first moment he met me. He

probably was far less aware of the extent of that need than was
I."

"The bastard," Brady repeated, reliving the attack on
Alison, and again feeling that awful psychic attack on himself,
the throttling hands, the weight of the beast upon him . . .

And it had been George Campbell, coldly and dispas-
sionately killing him, having helped to rob him of the family
he loved.

He said, calming down, "He was actually on the station
when the Watcher came into my lab and killed my experimen-
tal animals. He couldn't have been more than a hundred yards
from me."

Ellen nodded, as if she understood exactly what he meant.
"Most likely a pre-manifest. Campbell was in the process of
creating the elemental that would later attack so savagely.
Some residual, or side energy, created a minor form of
Watcher that targeted on you. He probably didn't even know
he had done it."

Brady stared at her, then shook his head in angry exaspera-
tion. "How the hell do you know so much? Every other sentence you speak is a fucking mini-lecture."

She watched him peculiarly. "Don't take it out on me. I'm
in no mood."

"Your expertise is almost suspicious. At times."

"I went *into* my work," she snapped pointedly. "You obviously weren't as keen." Brady was silent, his lips pressing
together, his eyes narrowed, the tension in his body almost intolerable. Ellen went on, "Everything about these attacks sug-
gests a source without total control. Remember what you
heard the collector say? 'Is Wickhurst a strong enough source?'
They had slight doubts about him even then. I'd go so far as to
say that Campbell transmits without always meaning to. The
elemental has taken control of him. It generates on its
own, drawing only from his unconscious desires. That's why
its attacks on me have gone so far and no further . . ."

"Even the first attack?"

Ellen grimaced and shook her head. "No. That was real
enough."

Brady picked up the shotgun, broke it open, then snapped it
shut again, cradling it in his two hands. "Reality," he said.

"Thank you for reminding me."

"What are you going to do?" She sat up and rubbed her eyes.

"What the hell do you think I'm going to do?" Brady reached for his jacket, and pushed the box of cartridges into the pocket. As he pulled the coat over his shoulders, so Ellen grasped his intention.

"You're not going to face Campbell now!"

"Why not? What better way to solve our problem and get a little extra information on where to start our search? Are you coming?"

Ellen faced him, and reached out to drag him back as he paced towards the door. "What the hell's the matter with you, Dan?"

"Nothing! I'm going to kill Campbell!"

"Wonderful! You blow his head off, and languish in Pentonville for fifteen years."

"They'll have to catch me first. Campbell will know *something* about where they've taken Alison. And he'll tell . . .'"

"Why should he? You walk in there, waving a shotgun, accusing him of psychic attack. He'll laugh at you. The police will laugh at you, Dan, you've got it all back to front." He glared at her, but she wouldn't let go of his arm. "Think, for Christ's sake, Dan. *Think.* You've got no evidence, no proof, nothing tangible at all. And Campbell, for all that I've just said, is not a weak man."

"Nor am I."

"Don't be so fucking arrogant!" Her voice had risen with anger. She deliberately calmed herself down. "What we need to do is *trap* Campbell. You can be sure that he'll be targeting for us, and sending a Stalker against us. He knows our defences, now, and he'll attack until he breaks through. We'll *let* him break through. Once in the house, we'll snare him. What the hell do you think all that's for?" She waved a hand towards the pile of boxes and objects on the table. Brady followed her glance, then looked back at her. "With his thought-form trapped, he'll be weak. He won't have the stamina to resist our questioning. Once we've got what *we* want, what *I* want, then and *only* then can you do what you like. Kill him and leave the search to me; or hand him over to the police and have a chance of hunting down the gathering party.''

The words sank in, and Brady gradually relaxed. The anger in him was subdued and he allowed himself a wry, bitter little smile. She was right, of course. It made no sense at all to go charging off to George Campbell's Buckinghamshire house at six in the morning. It would be asking for complications. He broke the shotgun and turned back into the dining room, walked to the table and picked up a mirror, its glass surface streaked with silver and green paint. Turning to stare at Ellen, who stood, arms folded, watching him, he waved the mirror in the air. "I've no idea how it works, but let's start building.''

"*You* start building,'' she said with a tired smile. "Wake me when the sun clears the top of the trees.''

Four o'clock in the afternoon.

The early morning frost had vanished quickly beneath the bright March sun, but the day had remained cold. By noon the clouds had begun to build up from the west, and rain threatened. This was a miserable and chilly sample of spring weather, more reminiscent of autumn. The wind gusted through the garden, occasionally sending a flurry of rain silently against the windows of Brook's Corner. But though the storm-clouds deepened, the heavy rain stayed off.

Ellen finished her psychic snare, and stood within it, her fingers crossed.

To Brady, the snare seemed remarkably simple, and very fragile: the shape of a pentangle, about six feet across had been made with thin, gold thread, the fifth angle pointing away from the garden doors. Inside that fifth angle had been placed the small, green mirror, its glass surface patterned with silver in the complex form of a triple spiral. Between the silver, the glass had also been painted green. At the shoulders of the pentagram, the gold thread had been coiled four times around large fragments of quartz. Inside the bottom angles, near the garden, were bone-handled copper daggers, their blades marked with the symbols of the Eye and of Venus. A dark un- guent, smelly and mucoid, was then dabbed at each angle: this consisted of a preparation of the flowers of wolf-bane, viper's bugloss, orpine, cinquefoil and vervain, with the inevitable addition of organic material from both Brady and Ellen.

"The combination of these herbs will help to ward off and thus weaken the psychic substance of the Stalker, and then contain it once it has broken through. The green, the copper, the four coils, are part of the symbolism of Venus, the planet of love and friendship. It's Mars—anger, hatred—that is coming against us. We fight *like* with *opposite*. We oppose hate with the idea of love, death with the idea of life. Okay? Simple enough?"

"Oh sure!"

"Last job," she said to Brady, handing him a long, iron knife. "Go and cut the maze outside the French windows."

"Cut the maze?" Brady took the knife, surprised at the weight of it. He pulled an anorak on as he stepped carefully across the gold thread and opened the windows.

"Three straight lines," Ellen instructed him, "running across the pattern, and meeting at the window step."

A channel, she explained, a way for the thought-form to pass through the first maze, before becoming ensnared in the second.

Brady bent his back to the task, sawing through the thick turf in as straight a line as possible. He had just finished the second cut, and was crouching on the lawn to begin the third, when he heard a car draw up around the front of the house. Still holding the knife he walked round to investigate. He was not at all happy to meet Bill and Rosemary Suchock.

"Hell, Dan," Bill said, almost nervously. He was swathed in a thick car coat, and holding Rosemary's hand. She stared at Brady through large, red-rimmed eyes. She had been crying. She looked like a small, lost child, being brought home.

"I'm sorry if I upset you," she said, her voice little more than a whisper.

"That's all right," said Brady. "I wasn't upset. I thought you were quite right to say what you did."

"Well I don't agree," said Suchock stiffly, and his brow creased into a frown, more of confusion than anger. "We've not been as close as we should. We've let concern for ourselves stop us being concerned for you. Good God, Dan, you've been through hell. The least we could do is stand by you, try and understand what's going on with you."

Of all the times to have an attack of conscience, Brady thought wryly. Ellen's words seemed to shout at him again: Rosemary is dangerous to have around. Keep them away, for their sakes *and* ours.

"You've done too much already," Brady said, stepping forward to take Bill's arm. He gently propelled them back towards their car. "When certain things are settled, when I'm more settled in myself again, I'll explain a lot to you. Right now, why not go home . . .?"

It was too patronizing, too obviously wrong. Suchock wriggled free of Brady's grip and turned on him, almost angrily. Rosemary went pale, stepped back and began to shiver as her husband said, "What the hell's all this about? You were only too glad of my help a few days ago. We've come round here to make amends for our cowardice. I admit I ran away. I was bloody terrified. But we're family, Dan. You and Rosemary and I. We're part of the same family, and we should stick together."

Suchock's face was infused with blood, his cheeks and forehead red with anger. He looked all of his forty-five years, a man with high blood pressure, an unfit man, drab and settled in his ways.

Brady said firmly, "This place is dangerous, Bill. I don't want you here, either of you. I'm expecting *company*. Do you understand what I mean? A job, begun at Christmas, has to be finished now. This place is not safe for anyone, and I don't want you here. I don't want to risk your lives too!"

It got through to Bill Suchock, who looked quite stunned. Perhaps it really had taken this long for Brady's true situation to sink in.

"You mean those men . . . those people might attack you again? Is it them who blew up the fence?"

Rosemary was instantly ill at ease. Her drawn features turned even paler. She huddled inside her raincoat, eyes darting about the grounds as if she sensed the danger already.

And as Brady said, "That's right . . ." so he sensed the danger too!

Suchock began to say, "Well, get the bloody police to put a few men inside. That's what they're here for . . ." He stopped speaking as he saw the look on Brady's face. "What is it?"

It was here! It was outside the wall, close to the front gate!
How he knew was not something that concerned him, now. He
could *feel* its presence watching him, watching the three of
them. Distantly, bells tinkled. There was a faint, eerie sound,
like the cracking of branches, a sound that went on and on,
even though it varied in intensity.

He heard Ellen's cry of "Dan! It's here!"

"What's here?" stuttered Suchock, his eyes widening in
panic. Rosemary, sensing only the danger, began to scream.

Brady tugged at them both. "Back to the house. Quick!"

As if in a daze, Bill Suchock stumbled after Brady, but
Rosemary began to run towards the front gate, along the
winding driveway until she was hidden by trees. Suchock realized that his wife wasn't with them and turned to chase after
her. Brady yelled at him not to be a fool, then raced along the
drive himself, slowing as he realized that Bill had stopped.

The gates in the high brick wall were being flung open and
shut, almost too fast for the eye to see. The hinges creaked,
the sound of the metal edges meeting became a persistent ringing. Rosemary stood there, staring at the gates as they were
blown back and forth with astonishing speed.

Finally the left hand gate broke from its hinges, and was
slung with a great crash onto the driveway. Gravel sprayed out
in a wide arc, and the fragments that struck Rosemary seemed
to mobilize her into some sort of action.

She screamed and began to run.

"Rosemary! Get to the house!"

Brady's cry echoed through the late afternoon. Bill Suchock
stumbled after his wife, who instead of running to safety, was
racing around the side of the building. A piece of wood the
size of a brick struck Suchock a hefty blow on the side of the
head and he stopped, turning to stare at the gateway, blood
streaming from the gash on his temple. He seemed undecided
as to what to do, then with a last glance to where Rosemary
had vanished, he returned to Brady. Brady let him into the
house, realizing that Suchock was stunned almost out of his
wits. When he tried to speak only an unintelligible jumble of
words emerged.

Brady opened the back door and stepped out, just this side
of the mazon. Rosemary, hands on her head, was running like

an animal pursued, her screams loud and hysterical, quite uncontrolled. Brady called to her, and stepped into the mazon. At the sound of his voice she stopped, stared at him, eyes streaming with tears. Then a great gustling wind blew at her, bowling her backwards onto the ground. Light, or fire, seemed to flicker around her. The apple trees bent and swayed in the storm, their branches whipping at the earth below them.

"Run to the house!" Brady again shouted, and stepped even further towards his sister.

The thought-form was almost at her. Brady could smell it. His gaze was drawn to the place where it stood, just inside the brick wall. There were no visible signs of it, but the drifting smoke from the nearest brazier seemed to coil and writhe about the insubstantial form that lurked there.

Rosemary picked herself up from the ground. She saw Brady and started to come towards him, and her face was open, panic-stricken, her mouth moving silently, now, in a plea for help. A second later she stopped, seemed to look up and around her, her hands waving pointlessly about. She was at the edge of the *zona magnetica*, trying to step forward. But she couldn't move. She edged to the side, and slowly the expression on her face turned to one of fearful terror. "I can't move . . . " she whined, and her voice became loud, "I can't move . . . I can't get through . . ."

What the hell was she talking about?

Brady stepped further forward. Only a few yards separated them. He would drag her into the house by force.

Ellen's sudden touch on his shoulder startled him. "Leave her."

"What d'you mean, leave her? I can't just leave her."

Ellen's whispered voice was urgent, edged with panic. "She's stuck, Dan. She can't break the psychic barrier. Can't you see that? Her reason has gone, and she's trapped there as effectively as if she were a thought-form herself!"

"What?" Brady's horrified cry was almost drowned by a sudden, deafening *cracking* sound, like the splitting of a thick beam of timber, but far more explosive. It had not been thunder. Cold rain began to sleet down from the miserable grey skies, blowing hard and icy against him. Rosemary raised her hands and stared at the water falling on them, touched her

suddenly drenched hair, as if she could hardly believe what was happening.

Something to her right startled her. She began to back away from whatever she could see, hands raised before her in a feeble attempt at self-protection. Then she sobbed, loudly and passionately, the sob more scream than sorrow. Turning, she began to flee. Brady thought he glimpsed an immense grey shape loping after her, wolverine but upright, and with the broad, mongoloid face of the drooling, dead-featured human that he had seen before. The vision had been fleeting, the sensation of a sleek grey shape, its legs effortlessly carrying it towards the running, bedraggled woman.

"I can't let this happen!" Brady cried, and began to break through the various zones around the house, pursuing his sister, blind to the danger, not even knowing how to defend himself against the Stalker.

He had taken just ten paces when Rosemary's raincoat was torn from her shoulders, and four great rents appeared in her clothing. A second later her body was whipped up into the air, then flung forty yards across the garden, into the branches of the tall oak, where it wedged between two gnarled limbs, a limp rag doll, its arms and legs still twitching, face staring blindly.

Brady felt sick with shock. It had happened so fast. He backed away from where he knew the thought-form to be. The smouldering herbs in the braziers irritated his senses, even through the light, cold rain. He stumbled on the edge of the turf maze outside the French windows, then realized that the Stalker was coming rapidly towards him.

Ellen's sudden hold on him was powerful, unrelenting. She dragged him into the cold lounge of the house, making him step round the gold wire. They stood at the back of the room and watched as the psychic substance of George Campbell's mind moved quickly through the French windows and began to dissipate, spreading out to seek those it needed to kill.

A moment later it had entered the gold and coppered pentagram. There was an unearthly screech, neither animal, nor human. Brady thought he could see a vaguely human shape struggling to get out of the confining space of the pentangle. The face that he glimpsed was dead, its tiny eyes dulled as it looked at him. The mouth was a simple gash, glistening in the pallid flesh, opening and closing, a reptilian horror created as much by his own fear as by the man who was projecting it. There were a number of air shocks, explosive decompressions that sucked the air from Brady's lungs. The room filled with a sweet, sickly odour, which vanished as quickly as it had appeared. There was a dull thump behind Brady, and when he glanced round he saw that the plaster and brick of the wall by the hallway door had been dented to a depth of several inches. Across the lounge, a window exploded outwards. "Random energy!" Ellen shouted, crouching as something struck the wall beside her, and caused a crack to appear from ceiling to floor.

Within the pentagram, the chaos stopped. There was emptiness and silence, and yet Brady felt a strong sense of unease. It was an unnatural stillness; it wasn't right.

"Ellen. Wait," he said, but Ellen waved him silent, stepping gingerly forward, towards the trap. Brady stepped forward too, his hands held out from his body, the attitude of a man ready to run at the slightest danger. He peered into the face of the mirror and saw that the silvered coating was scratched and marked, as if by claws.

"Gotcha!" Ellen said with a frail smile, and glanced at Brady. Her eyes radiated triumph. "We've got it. Trapped. We've got Campbell."

"I don't like it," Brady said. "I'm uneasy."

"With what? It's trapped. There . . ." she stabbed at the mirror. "Its random energy has been expended. It'll decay naturally, over the course of a few hours."

She stood and made to step into the pentagram to pick the mirror up.

"No! Ellen!"

Brady's cry came too late. She was half across the gold wire, glancing curiously at him, when her body was suddenly flung upwards, against the ceiling, with a sound like a thunder-clap.

"OH GOD!" was all she managed, a desperate cry, sudden awareness, and sudden death, combined into a shriek of pure terror. Her face turned as black as soot. Brady reached to her, his mouth open in shock, his mind numbed.

He tried to reach *out* of his body, to grapple the thought-form as he had fought it once before—

For a fleeting second he was aware of the shapeless mass
that was killing the woman, felt a transient touch of mind on
mind. But it was too late, and he could not control the talent
sufficiently.

"ELLEN!"

He heard bones snap. There was a sound like flesh being
struck. Her eyes bulged in the blackened flesh of her face, lips
drew back in terrible pain. He heard two gasps, strangled
words. "Mirror . . . silk . . ."

And then she was silent, ceasing to struggle. Her body
struck the floor and lay there without moving, its face turned
away from Brady, who collapsed to his knees, staring at the
dead girl, the tears welling up in his eyes.

Random energy, a last assault before the snare took it fully,
whatever it had been, it had gone now. The room was filled
with an intense calm.

"One mistake . . ." Brady murmured through his stifled
sobs, and shook his head. "One mistake . . ."

He looked towards the French windows. The rain was still
falling, blown by the gusting wind. He could see Rosemary's
torn raincoat lying on the saturated grass.

And he could hear a distant whimpering: the half-conscious
sobbing of the broken woman who was his sister.

SEVENTEEN

THE PAIN BEGAN and he knew at once that something had gone wrong. The sensation in his skull and stomach were totally unfamiliar to him. In his skull, it was like the closing down of a camera shutter, a tremendous pressure applied to the tissues. In his stomach it was as if fingers delved among his organs, twisting and knotting the tubes and lobes of his viscera.

The intangible umbilical cord that connected with his thought-form stretched out before him, and seemed to shrivel and wither, the life force between mind and elemental strangled and blocked.

He sat in the darkness and allowed himself to emit two shrill, brief screeches of agony, eyes squeezed shut, breath bursting from his body with such pressure that, following each cry, he felt a moment's relief.

What could possibly have happened?

Slowly he reached for the light. The illumination of his small room allowed him to see that all was normal. The coloured patterns before him, the mannikins, the clay images, the iron talisman, the names of power written in wax on the intricate symbol of Mars.

But within the last twenty seconds the thought-form, the most powerful projection he had ever conjured, had become lost from him.

It was just not possible!

He had experienced nothing like this ever before. The elemental always drained back to him, renewing him, revitalizing his tiring body. But now, he sensed that the elemental was *lost*.

His hand shook. The pain in his skull grew more unbearable. The edges of his vision began to crowd in, making the room seem darker than it was. He knew that saliva was dripping from his parted lips, but he no longer had the strength to raise a hand and wipe his mouth.

I'm dying . . .

And through the agony of physical discomfort, and rapidly ensuing unconsciousness, the thought came to him that if the loss of his vital energy didn't kill him, the mandrathon would. Even now he could hear the rapid clicking, and the rhythmic chinking sound, like metal on metal, that told of the nearness of a targeting psychic force.

I'm beyond help . . .

Judith was in Norfolk. She had not wanted to go, but he had insisted, making more excuses than should have been credible. She had gone and he was alone in the house. Beyond help.

His thoughts became confused. His vision had narrowed until he could hardly see. The mandrathon approached, and he knew—it was among the last coherent thoughts he managed —that it would see at once how he had failed.

Such a simple task. So simple a task to accomplish. How is it possible that I failed so badly?

The noise of the thought-form increased. His limbs felt paralysed, the pressure in his skull more than intolerable, but there was no strength left to scream. Distantly, as he sank further into oblivion, he heard the sound of footsteps on the stairs. The room shook, a cool breeze touched his skin. Someone—or some thing—had burst into his haven, battering down the door to get to him.

As he jerked his head back, lolling helplessly in his chair, he saw a familiar figure through the greyness, the figure of a man, leaning close, reaching out to him . . .

It was Daniel Brady.

Here, in the house! Brady!

And he knew, then, that his doom was sealed.

• • •

The stench was appalling.

Brady fought his rising gorge, willing himself not to vomit. Campbell had been doubly incontinent, and his shirt front was spattered with pale vomit. Brady could scarcely believe that this broken, dying thing was his Director, and a man whose mental power had been at war with him for many weeks.

Clearly, the man was being killed. There were bruise marks on his face, and his eyes were swollen, almost completely closed. His mouth gaped, the tongue protruding slightly. He had collapsed in his chair, and he seemed to regard Brady as he sprawled there, but Brady could not believe that anything much in the way of reason was left in this shattered man.

He placed the shotgun on the table, among the bizarre trinkets and talismans of Campbell's secret trade. Leaning down he slapped Campbell's face twice, trying to revive some spark of consciousness.

Behind the puffed lids, Campbell's eyes glittered. He was watching the man he had tried to kill.

"Campbell! Can you hear me? Campbell!" He wanted to kill him, to throttle him, to take the gun and smash the drooling face to a pulp.

But he wanted an answer first.

Dropping to a crouch, desperately trying to put the agony of the stench out of his awareness, Brady held Campbell's head between his hands and shouted at him: "My family! My children! Are they alive? Tell me! Tell me, damn you. Are they still alive?"

Campbell's mouth moved. Saliva dripped, and bubbled on his lips. Brady shook the man's head. "Are they alive? Tell me!"

Sound came from the man's throat, a gurgling, incoherent murmur. Brady leaned close, desperate to hear the words. If Campbell was resisting him even now, then by God he *would* smash the man's skull.

There was something in the room, something watching; he could smell something sharp, like the mandrake braziers . . . it was a Stalker, it had to be. But who was it after?

"My children. Answer me, Campbell. For the love of God, there's nothing I can do for you now. I beg you, help me.

Answer me. Where are they? Are they alive?"

And this time as he listened to the dying breath of the man, he heard the word, "Alive . . ." repeated twice.

Brady felt tears sting his eyes. It *had* to be true. Dear God, please let it be true.

He stared at Campbell. "Are you sure! Are they truly alive?"

As if summoning the last vestiges of strength, Campbell nodded his head. His left hand raised from the arm of the chair and fell heavily on Brady's wrist. The fingers clutched convulsively. Campbell's eyes widened slightly, and Brady could see that the whites were congested with blood, the pupils narrowed to mere pin-pricks.

"Where are they held? Tell me that? Where is my family now?"

"North . . ." murmured the dying man, the spittle bubbling on his lips and making the word hard to hear. "North . . . rach . . . nee . . . all . . . live . . . not . . . long . . . Brady . . . fail . . . kill . . ."

"What are you saying, Campbell? I don't understand! They're alive, but not for long? Is that what you said?"

"Mandrath . . . attack . . ."

"I don't understand!" Growing frustration. The presence in the room was almost tangibly threatening. "Who took my family?"

Campbell forced himself upright and his face came close to Brady's. His foul breath made Brady wince, but Brady stayed close, willing Campbell to say more.

"Arach . . . awakening . . ." gasped the dying man. "They've . . . come back . . . power . . . no time . . ."

"I don't understand! Campbell, I don't understand! Are my family alive but not for long? Is that what you mean?"

Campbell fell back. The hand on Brady's wrist slipped away. Brady thought he heard the word "yes" whispered, and then a peculiar whining sound began to issue from Campbell's glistening mouth. His hands convulsively slapped to his head. He jerked bolt upright in the chair. His eyes bulged and he began to screech.

Brady stood and backed away. The room had become icily cold, and the walls . . . the walls seemed to be melting.

In alarm, feeling the panic surfacing inside him, he looked around at the way the plaster seemed to be dripping from the walls. The desk was melting too, the objects on it flowing and distorting out of their true shapes. The ceiling drooped in the middle, threatening to crash down upon the two men in the room.

Brady stepped to the door quickly. Campbell's screaming reached its highest pitch and the man stood, fists clenched against the sides of his head, which suddenly began to peel, the flesh tearing away from the bone in ragged strips, like a pink banana. The skull still stared; the hands were twisted and snapped, bones crushed audibly.

Brady raised the shotgun and emptied both barrels into the face of the bloody-boned horror that had once been a man.

Then he turned and fled, from the house, through the garden with its well-concealed defences, across the low brick wall at the bottom, and to his car, parked discreetly a hundred yards away.

Behind him he heard an explosion and saw flame begin to lick high into the dusk sky.

—EPILOGUE————

AFTER HE HAD dismantled the trap, he picked up the green and silvered mirror and toyed with the idea of smashing it. But Ellen's last words had referred to "silk", and he went upstairs to the main bedroom, seeking among Alison's clothes for the black silk scarf he had bought for her some years ago. He tied the scarf around the small mirror, completely covering the face. Then he lay it flat, on the dressing table, and as if he felt it would help he placed a heavy book on top of it.

He didn't know what else to do.

Bill Suchock rang from the hospital. He was upset, still very shaken. Rosemary was physically out of danger, broken bones and very bad lacerations to her upper torso. She would pull through all right.

Physically.

"I don't know what to say, Bill."

"Say nothing, then. Just pray for her. Pray for her mind. You haven't forgotten how to pray, have you?"

"No," said Brady. "I haven't forgotten that."

A little after he carried Ellen's body up to the bedroom. He no longer cared about the police, or moving the evidence. He felt more than slightly lost without the woman. She had known so much, she had crammed her mind with so much research, during her months of seclusion.

And now he had lost her, and he was alone again. And he had lost that touch of love, the growing bud of affection, that might have helped soothe the agonies of the search to come.

And perhaps in a way that was good. He might have become complacent in Ellen's company. In time he might have lost the edge, and the hunt might never have been completed.

He had very little to go on, but he had one thing that was more important than everything else put together.

His family was still alive. He would not believe otherwise. Alison, Marianna, Dominick—whatever the purpose in abducting them, that purpose had not yet been achieved—they were being taken to the north, and they were still alive, and he would find them if it took him until the end of the century!

He had a house that was strongly—if not completely —defended against any further psychic attack. He had a rudimentary knowledge of what he was dealing with, and that knowledge would increase. He had images: of a face, of an amulet; of a maze; memories of two voices that had spoken above his recumbent body; he had names: Arachne, Magondathog, Lazarine, Awakening. None of them might mean anything at all. Any one of them might lead him to the "Collectors" who had visited Brook's Corner on a dark, cold evening three months before, and taken his whole life, his whole future.

He walked distractedly around the house, hands thrust into his pockets, unsure of what to do. He hid the shotgun as thoroughly as he could, then walked around the garden, checking the zones of defence. He propped the broken front gate against its hinges, and listened to the still, silent night, he didn't know for what.

There was an expectancy in him, a sense of waiting, but it defied all reason. He was at once calm, and yet on edge. There was something further to happen. He couldn't think what.

And then, at two in the morning, the house began to whisper to him. It was an incoherent murmur, more hallucinatory than real. At first it frightened him, then puzzled him. He went upstairs to the bedroom, and the whispering was stronger. It formed no words, and yet it was a voice. A woman's voice.

He went to bed and lay down next to the body of Ellen Bancroft, not afraid to turn and look at her choked, bruised features. He turned his head to the right and stared at the concealed mirror. The whispering grew a little louder.

After an hour or so he began to smile, even though his heart
was racing, his body shaking with a touch of fear, a great deal
of excitement.

He began to understand what was going on. The thought-
form would decay from the trap—Ellen had hinted as much
before she had died—but there was a more vital, more animate
ghost left in the house, and it had remained there by its own
choice.

Contented, feeling strengthened, he closed his eyes to try to
sleep.

He was not as totally alone as he had thought.

Ellen had decided to stay around for a while.

*The girl was crying again. It was a persistent, irritating sound,
and the man who guarded her paced the caravan restlessly, re-
gretting bitterly that the family had been divided. When the
three of them had been together they had huddled, comfortable in each other's presence. The mother had screamed at the
guardian, shouting abuse, but at least there had not been this
continuous, unearthly sobbing.*

*The sooner it was done the better; the sooner the girl was
used, the better. The girl had power, talent. That would be
taken from her first, before she was sent north, with the
others, to be used during the awakening.*

*This time of gathering had gone on too long; the man was
impatient to go north, for the time of change.*